# THE PROFESSOR'S LADY

HOLLY BUSH

Copyright © 2021 by Holly Bush

All rights reserved.

No part of this book may be reproduced in any form or by any electronic or mechanical means, including information storage and retrieval systems, without written permission from the author, except for the use of brief quotations in a book review.

❦ Created with Vellum

# CHAPTER 1

Philadelphia Harbor, July 1870

"Wait," Kirsty Thompson shouted as she hurried across the deck of the steamer *Maybelle*. "Wait! Stop!"

A uniformed man with sideburns that reached his chin turned from directing sailors. "Miss?"

"You must stop moving the boat," she said breathlessly, coming to a halt in front of him.

"It's a steamer ship, not a boat," he said.

"It doesn't matter what you call it, you must stop—set the brake or whatever you must do—because I need to get off."

"I'm sorry, miss. The lines have been pulled. We'll be underway any moment now."

"But I must get off," Kirsty repeated, feeling a rising panic.

The man eyed her. "Where's your ticket, miss?"

"I . . . I don't have one."

"Then how did you get aboard?" he asked, hands on his hips.

"There was a woman going up the ramp ahead of me, a rather

large woman with a flowered dress that nearly blinded me, with a little dog, a child, and three or four servants."

"And you walked in with her. Hiding amongst her party," he said. "You didn't want to pay passage, and you thought you'd sneak aboard."

"Of course not! I'm no thief! I just needed to speak to someone. Just for a moment, I needed to speak to him."

"Lovers gone bad?" the man said and turned away to shout at a sailor. He turned back and regarded her. "Well, you're stuck on this ship with him now."

"Lovers! How dare you! I am not with him or anyone, and that is why I need to get off!"

"You can get off in New York harbor because that's our next stop," the man shouted back at her.

"New York? I don't want to go to New York!" Kirsty stepped closer to the man and wagged a finger at him. "And you are being rude with your shouting!"

"Now see . . ."

"Miss Thompson?"

Kirsty turned quickly. "Oh, Mr. Watson. I've been looking for you! Please tell this man to stop the boat and let me off!" The steamer lurched from its moorings, and Kirsty would have tumbled to her knees if it hadn't been for Mr. Watson catching her by the elbows. She'd been introduced to him by her brother-in-law when she'd attended a party held at her sister's home. He'd escorted her to dinner on that evening. She was so happy he remembered her!

"I'm af-fraid," he said. "That will be impos-sible. We're under-way, it seems."

"Oh no," she said and looked up at him, feeling tears gather in her eyes. She didn't want to cry. Her family accused her occasionally of crying to get her way, which was hardly ever the case and certainly wasn't now. But she dare not blink, or those tears she did not want to cry would tumble down her cheeks.

"Perhaps a cup of t-tea would help you, Miss Thompson. Allow me to take you to the d-d-dining room."

"But I must get off this boat," she said. "My family won't have any idea where I've gone and . . . and they will be so worried." That was no exaggeration. They would assume the worst.

"I don't b-believe there is anything we can do until we land at New York harbor," he said and held out his arm.

Kirsty wrapped her arm around his and looked up at him. He was such a tall man with dark hair, very green eyes, and burning cheeks. "Oh. Oh no. I've embarrassed you with my shouting. Your face is quite red. I am so sorry. Please don't be angry."

He shook his head. "I'm not angry," he said very slowly.

Kirsty turned as he did toward the doors leading to the inside hallways after glancing longingly at the dock, now getting smaller as they moved from shore. He seated her at a table once they were in the dining room, signaled a waiter, and nodded at her to order. She opened her drawstring bag to see what amount of money she had left after paying for the trolley that day. She was suddenly panicked when she realized she'd have to find a way to travel to Philadelphia from New York when this infernal boat stopped, and she'd need money to do it.

"Nothing for me, thank you," she said to the waiter.

"I'll have coffee and this assortment of cheese and olives listed on your menu," he said. "The lady will have tea. Thank you."

She leaned forward. "I don't have enough money to pay for it. Surely they'll give me a glass of water."

"Miss T-Thompson, I will take care of the b-bill. Please don't worry." He raised his hand as if he was calling to the waiter again.

But a young—very young—red-haired man walked to their table instead. His face had an unsightly burn scar on one side, and Kirsty did her best not to look at it as he arrived at the table. She wondered how Mr. Watson knew him.

"Clawson," Watson said. "Change of plans. You'll need to contact the Royal Academy and see about rescheduling my talk."

"Yes, sir, right away, sir."

"We'll be staying in New York tomorrow evening. We'll need three rooms at the hotel where we often stay."

"Three rooms, sir?"

"One for you, one for me, and one for Miss Thompson." He nodded to her. "Clawson, this is Miss Thompson. Miss Thompson, my assistant, Mr. Clyde Clawson."

"A hotel room? Oh no! I'll be heading directly home. I have to get home. My family will be frantic!"

"Miss Thompson, I d-doubt we'll be able to catch a train after we arrive as it will be very late in the day. We'll have to wait until the next morning to travel."

"How do you know? Do you always take a steamer to New York? Isn't it easier to catch the train?"

"Ah," Clawson said. "I'll need to see if our tickets can be canceled or sold, perhaps."

Kirsty watched the young man hurry away. "What did he mean about the tickets being sold? What tickets?"

Mr. Watson stared at her and then looked up at the waiter bringing their cheese platter and pots of coffee and tea. He pulled bills out of his wallet, handed them to the waiter, and told him to keep the change. He stirred several sugar cubes into the cup of coffee the waiter poured for him and looked up at her.

"Tickets for a t-transatlantic crossing."

"Why would you cancel your tickets? When were you planning on sailing?" she asked, interested to know if the date could work for her, although after she arrived home the day after tomorrow, she doubted if her older sister and brother, Muireall and James, would ever let her out of their sight again.

"The day after tomorrow, Miss T-Thompson. This steamer stops in New York to pick up additional p-p-passengers and then goes directly to England."

"Well, why can't you go now? Has something happened?"

He stared at his cup for some time. He would prefer to

continue to England as planned but he could not abandon her without an escort. And spending time with this beautiful, vivacious woman would not be a hardship. "I can hardly allow you to t-travel by yourself, Miss Thompson. I will see you back to your home."

Kirsty shook her head. "No. Oh no. You mustn't. I could not allow you to change your plans on my account."

"Have some r-refreshments, Miss Thompson. We will not arrive until tomorrow afternoon."

Kirsty felt the blood rushing to her cheeks. "I thank you for the tea, and I will see that you are repaid once we are home in Philadelphia. But you cannot tell me what to do, Mr. Watson. You are not my father or brother or any relation."

He leaned forward. "I am, however, a gentleman, and you are related to my good friend Mr. Pendergast, your brother-in-law, in fact. I could not countenance any young lady traveling alone if it was in my power to prevent it, especially as she is related to my circle of friends."

"You are not stuttering, Mr. Watson." Kirsty put a hand over her mouth as if doing so would stop her rude words from being heard. "I'm so sorry. I should never have mentioned it."

He shrugged. "Stuttering or not, I will escort you home."

"My family . . ." she began and trailed off, thinking of how terrified they would be when she did not arrive home for supper.

"We will send a t-telegram as soon as we arrive at the hotel."

"You don't understand."

"Will you explain it to me?"

ALBERT WATCHED AS SHE SAT QUIETLY FOR SEVERAL MINUTES, sipping her tea and staring at the spoon she'd used to stir in her sugar, turning it over slowly. She looked up at him finally with a resolved, or resigned, serious look on her face that he did not understand from this young woman. He'd been introduced to her and had escorted her into dinner at the home of his friend Alexander Pendergast, who was married to her sister. She had been a frivolous whirlwind of chatter that evening after getting over some initial nervousness, but neither persona had stopped him from finding her the most beautiful woman of his acquaintance, with a joyous laugh that went straight to his gut. However, he was certain she would find nothing remotely interesting about him or his medical research, or the fact that sometimes he forgot to eat. His colleagues called his work brilliant. His mother called him a scatterbrain.

"There are men who want to harm us," she said. "Did you know that my sister Elspeth was kidnapped before she married Alexander? She was! She was taken from us at a grand ball at Alexander's family home."

Albert shook his head, hoping she would explain. She leaned close to him, close enough that he could smell lilacs or some other aromatic that seemed to wrap around him, yet he could feel her panic.

"My father was the Earl of Taviston in Scotland. There was a man, an illegitimate cousin, who claimed the earldom was his, and he tried to kill my mother, stole my younger brother from us, thankfully he was rescued, and lobbied the governors who oversee such things to give him the title and the wealth and the lands. My father was so concerned about the danger to his family that he brought us to America, hoping to wait in safety until everything was settled and Plowman, the cousin, was jailed. But they murdered my father and mother on the passage here," she hissed. "They poisoned their food, and my parents were buried at sea."

She had tears and terror in her eyes as she whispered to him, as if there were enemies all around.

"Why did they kidnap Mrs. P-Pendergast?"

"An exchange! They wanted us to turn over my brother Payden, the heir to the earldom," she said with a trembling lip.

"Elspeth knew her duty, though. She would die for him, as would any of us."

"Die for him?"

"Had Alexander and my brother James not rescued her, she would have been . . . abused and murdered as we would never turn the rightful Earl of Taviston over to them."

Albert sat back in his chair and stared at her. Good God! What a story!

"Isn't James the oldest brother?" he said, remembering the looks he'd gotten from the man as he'd escorted his sister into dinner that night. He was a boxer—and a champion too.

"James? He is actually a cousin. His parents died when he was an infant; his mother was my father's sister. Mother and Father took him in and raised him as their own."

"But he's not your true b-broth—"

She'd leaned across the table again, but there were no tears this time, only a look that would have scared the most seasoned sailor. "James Thompson is my brother."

He nibbled on some cheese and a cracker and pushed the platter to her side of the table. "So your family will assume something s-similar has happened to you."

She nodded. "When will we arrive in New York?"

"By tomorrow afternoon." He gave her a frank look. "Why did you come aboard?"

Her face reddened, like a length of pink gauze was slowly creeping up from the base of her neck. "Well," she looked at her hands, "I was hoping to talk to you."

"T-To me? Whatever for?"

"Alexander said that you travel to England regularly for your medical work, and I was hoping you'd agree to escort me and a companion." She looked up. "I plan to import fine Scottish wool and yarns to America. I believe Thompson Wools and Yarn would be quite successful. I need to go to Scotland and meet the people I've been corresponding with about such a venture."

"Your brother would never allow it."

"No. But there would be nothing he could do if I boarded with my companion while they read a letter about my destination. Although I worried they'd be upset and frightened as they will, undoubtedly, be today."

"And you think I would have agreed to this outrageous scheme?"

"You aren't stuttering. Again."

"I find that I don't stutter when I am furious."

"Oh. What prompts it when you do stutter?"

He looked away. Miss Kirsty Thompson had the body of a siren, the face of an angel, and the scruples of the devil. He was, at the same time, horrified by her and attracted to her. Perhaps there was a medical explanation. And his stutter was especially prevalent when he was nervous. This young woman made his orderly, scholarly world tumble through the firmament.

# CHAPTER 2

"Would you l-like to take a turn about the deck, Miss Thompson?" Albert asked when their dishes had been cleared away. "The afternoon is warm, but there's always a breeze on the w-water."

They'd not said another word to each other as they drank their tea and coffee and nibbled on the food on the platter. Not after she'd asked him why he was stuttering. He could not tell her that her presence made him nervous and in turn made him trip over his words. When he'd taken her into dinner at the Pendergasts' those months ago and had been seated beside her, he'd said little, only opening his mouth to eat his food. Miss Thompson had carried the conversation without him, and he had been entranced.

"That would be very pleasant, Mr. Watson."

He followed her to the door and offered his arm when they were outside. She wrapped her hand around his elbow as they walked side by side, occasionally having to separate to walk single file when others passed on the narrow walkway. It was at one of those single-file moments that Miss Thompson nearly went overboard.

"Oof," she cried when a man in rough clothes bumped her toward the railing, but the barrier she was beside wasn't the same as most of the railing on the rest of the ship. She was pushed against a two-foot-wide gap strung with two loose lengths of chain and hooks, hung low, used when the boats docked to onboard supplies, he guessed.

Albert grabbed her by the waist, thankful that the ship was not rolling on waves and that his arms could reach her in time. He had an unpleasant vision of diving into the churning water to rescue her.

"Oh my dear Lord!" she cried as he pulled her back against his front and steadied himself with his hand wrapped around a pipe overhead. He felt her shuddering breath as she leaned against him, letting him take all of her weight. He glanced over his shoulder, looking for the man in the rough clothes and saw him round the corner with a look and a nod.

But it wasn't him the man had nodded at, he realized quickly. It was a well-dressed man walking past them just now.

"Miss! Be careful of your steps!" the man said with a solicitous air. "Allow me to escort you somewhere to sit down."

Watson pulled her back tight against him, his arm holding her flush to him as she took a breath to speak. "I'm the young lady's escort," he said.

Other passengers had gathered in the crowded area, many asking what had happened and pointing to the two loose chains. She was shaking against him as one woman recounted the event; she'd been walking behind them and had seen it all.

"Come," the well-dressed man said with a smile, his hand outstretched. "I'm sure you both would like to get somewhere less crowded. Follow me."

Watson turned, pulling her against his side, and headed the other direction, watchful as he made his way that he avoided the man in the rough clothes.

"Mr. Watson! Please slow down! I cannot keep up!"

"I need to get you to my stateroom," he said and looked down the narrow stairwell that led to his rooms.

"What? Oh no! I cannot go into your rooms. I cannot. Release me!" She turned to leave him and saw a face she recognized, a woman who was an acquaintance of her sister-in-law, and often on the society page of the *Philadelphia Inquirer*. Edith Fairchild was her name.

He took her by the shoulders and turned her to face him, taking little note of the other passengers around them. "Miss Thompson, settle yourself. The man who bumped you? That was not random. He pushed you. *You.*"

The blood drained from her face. "What are you saying?" she asked, quickly forgetting the woman now observing them.

"Come with me. Hurry now. Hold up your skirts. I don't want to trip on them as we descend."

She hurried down the steps, holding her dress up and away from the stairs. He stayed close to her as they went down the hallway and quickly opened the door to his room. He followed her inside, snicked both locks closed, and took a deep breath.

"What do you mean, he pushed me? It was just an accident, was it not?" Her words trailed to a whisper.

"I don't believe so," he said as he looked around the room, mostly consisting of a bed, a door to a small washroom, and another to Clawson's room.

Miss Thompson dropped down on to his bed, holding her small purse at her waist. "What do you believe?"

"I believe he pushed you on purpose."

"Perhaps he just lost his footing. Perhaps he was dizzy or drunk." She looked up. "Maybe you are seeing ghosts because of my family's story I'd just told you."

He shook his head. "There were two of them, Miss Thompson. The man who shoved you and the well-dressed man who asked you if he could help find you a seat."

She would not take his word until he explained everything he'd seen.

"I'm too terrified to move," she said finally.

"You don't have to move. We're staying right here in this room until we disembark tomorrow afternoon."

"My brother will be furious."

"I will be happy to explain to him that we had no other choice."

Her lip trembled. "I'm afraid he will hit you with his fists. He will hurt you."

"I'm sure Mr. Thompson will be reasonable, and in any case, I can take c-care of myself," he said.

"Not with James, you can't! You're taller for certain, but he's the champ. Not that it makes me think any less of you." She glanced away.

This woman could get under a man's skin like no other woman he'd ever met. She probably thought she was complimenting him when she'd said she wouldn't think any less of him, and he wasn't concerned about what she thought—was he?—and anyway, his best attribute was his analytical brain.

"I'm h-happy to hear that," he said. He walked to the door connecting the rooms and tapped. "Clawson?"

THE LOCK JIGGLED AND THE KNOB TURNED AS KIRSTY watched. Mr. Clawson entered, looked at her and back at Mr. Watson, his face turning red.

"I really can't countenance any sort of interlude with a young lady, Mr. Watson. I'll resign if you prefer," Clawson said.

"Good Lord, Clawson! I have no untoward designs on Miss Thompson! There's been an attempt on her life!"

"Oh." Clawson turned his attention to her. "Are you all right, miss? Shall I summon the captain?"

"We will handle this ourselves," Mr. Watson said. "With your p-permission, Miss Thompson."

She stared at him, glanced at Mr. Clawson, and back to Mr. Watson. They were honorable men. She knew it in her heart, and she did not believe that her brother-in-law, Alexander, would be friends with someone who was not a gentleman. "I don't want to involve anyone else. I just want to go home."

"Fine. I will get you home, Miss Thompson. I propose you and I stay here for the d-duration of the voyage, as uncomfortable as that may be, and allow Mr. Clawson to fetch us food for our meal."

"Whatever you think is best, Mr. Watson. I realize that as a female I would be easily overcome by men wishing me harm. I am truly sorry to involve you and Mr. Clawson in this, but I accept your protection. I need it," she said, trying to keep her voice from shaking.

"We will do our very best. For this evening, I will stay with Mr. Clawson, so you will have this r-room to yourself." He glanced at Clawson.

"Of course, sir."

"That is completely unnecessary. This is your room," she said.

He shook his head. "Mr. Clawson, I will see to removing my traveling bag to your room if you will go check on our trunks and make sure they will be off-loaded in New York."

Mr. Watson followed Mr. Clawson into the other room, and they spoke in low voices that she could not make out. She felt like the very biggest idiot ever to grace the city of Philadelphia. She was also scared out of her wits. When Mr. Watson had told her about the two men who appeared to be working in conjunction, she'd felt panic claw at her, and it was everything she could do not to become hysterical right there on the deck of the *Maybelle*, screaming for her brothers and sisters and for her great-aunt Murdoch, who'd come with them on the crossing and lived with them still. She heard the door close and the lock turn in the other cabin. Mr. Watson appeared in the doorway.

"Miss Thompson, you mustn't worry. Mr. Clawson and I will see you are s-safe."

She nodded. "You must not stand on my account. Sit down on the bed, or it will be a long evening."

Mr. Watson cleared his throat, and she watched the muscles in his neck move above the collar of his shirt. He was so very tall. Taller than James and even taller than their family's friend and James's cornerman, MacAvoy, and the top of her head only came up to *his* shoulder. She had to tilt her head back, as she was doing now, just to look at Mr. Watson's face. Maybe she'd thought him spindly and weak looking because he was so tall. But that was clearly not true. He had broad shoulders and long arms, which she was thankful for as he'd been able to save her from falling head over feet into the Atlantic Ocean. She closed her eyes and took a deep breath. She was not ready to meet her Maker.

"Mr. Clawson has gone to check our t-trunks and secure our evening meal. He will stay in the k-kitch . . . in the k-kitchens while our food is prepared. I told him about your p-parents' demise, and he will be d-diligent."

"Mr. Watson, you seem most upset." She looked at him with concern.

He rubbed his eyes with his thumb and forefinger and blew out a long, slow breath. "It would be m-most inappropriate to discuss."

"And why is that? We are private here in your stateroom, after all."

Mr. Watson shook his head and smiled at her in a way that made her think he thought her daft. "Mr. Clawson will r-return shortly," he said very slowly.

Kirsty stood and walked to him. She laid a hand on his arm. "Please don't be angry with me. I'm so very sorry."

"I'm not angry." He glanced at her hand.

"Well, it seems you are very angry. Although you did say you do not stutter when you are furious, but it seems to me—"

"Miss Thompson!" He reached out to her, holding her elbows. "It is highly inappropriate for us to be alone t-together and in a r-room that holds a b-bed as its singular piece of furniture!"

She looked up at him and blinked. "There is a small set of drawers there. The bed is not the only piece of furniture in the room."

"You d-don't understand."

"Then you must explain it to me. I am not feeble-minded."

He clutched her arms tightly. "You are a desirable woman, Miss Thompson. Very much so. And we are in a small room with just a bed."

"Oh," she said and felt the heat of a blush climb her cheeks. She'd been kissed a few times, but there had never been any type of spoken declaration. Just some fumbling wet lips and an occasional wandering hand that she was quite capable of managing thanks to her instructions from James. She glanced at the bed and back to his face, a handsome and intense face. "But you are a gentleman. I'm not afraid of you."

He swallowed. "I am. I am a gentleman, and I don't want you to ever have a fear of me. I would never harm you."

Kirsty relaxed and smiled up at him. "Then we will do fine until I am home."

Kirsty stretched out on the bed after she'd eaten some of the roast beef and buttered rolls that Mr. Clawson had brought them, hoping to relax and not think about the ocean churning directly in her sight as she'd leaned over the chain on the railing. Her eyes blinked open, and she realized she'd finally fallen asleep in a bed she did not think would be quite this comfortable. But something had awoken her, and a sound in the hallway made her sit up quickly and lurch to the door connecting the rooms.

"Mr. Watson?" she whispered, opened the door, and ran directly into his arms. They came around her protectively.

"Miss Thompson," he said, his voice strangled. "What is it?"

"I heard something. A scratching sound." She breathed in the scent of him that reminded her of the Locust Street house when the mantel was trimmed for the Christmas season. She closed her eyes and pressed her cheek against the smooth, warm cotton of his shirt.

He let go of her, hurried through the door to the adjoining room, and held his ear close to the door. Mr. Clawson did the same in the room she was in and then bent down to a leather satchel on floor. He rummaged through and pulled out a gun.

"Oh no, Mr. Clawson. You must not shoot anyone," she whispered.

"Mr. Watson has instructed me to guard you if he is unable to," he said, blushing. "And I am not of a size like Mr. Watson to be intimidating."

She glanced at Mr. Watson in the next room, his hand on the doorknob, and thought he was the least intimidating person she'd ever met. He turned it slowly, swung the door open, and disappeared into the hallway. She held her breath. He re-entered the room, turned the locks, and came through the connecting door.

"I don't see anyone in the hallway. You may put the pistol away, Mr. Clawson," he said. "I think we are very close to daylight. When we disembark this afternoon, I would like you to carry both of our satchels. I'd like to have my hands free to keep Miss Thompson close by."

"Certainly."

Watson turned to her. "Now if you'll excuse me, Miss Thompson, I am not f-fully clothed."

"Not fully clothed?" She took him in, from the top of his head to his feet, stopping briefly on the chest she'd laid her head on, her eyes flickering to his.

"I removed my shoes and vest when I laid down to sleep."

## THE PROFESSOR'S LADY

"Then you must sit, Mr. Watson."

"I cannot sit while a lady is standing."

"Oh, for heaven's sake," she said and plopped down on the edge of the bed, thinking how Aunt Murdoch would scold her for such a comment. "I am seated, sir." She looked down at his stockinged feet. "Goodness! You have large feet!"

Mr. Watson stared down at his feet while Mr. Clawson turned his back on the two of them, rearranging something in their leather bags, but she noticed his shoulders were shaking. Mr. Watson's face was bright red.

"T-Typically, tall persons' feet accommodate their height with l-length so that a person like myself doesn't tip over."

"Oh." She smiled up at him with a chuckle. "Of course! But yours are the biggest feet I've ever seen."

Mr. Watson sat down abruptly and turned away from her, sliding his feet into shoes and leaning down to tie the laces. Mr. Clawson held his vest as he stood and slid his arms through the opening, pulling it forward by the lapels, glancing at her as she watched him. This was different and so much more delightful than watching James or MacAvoy or her brother-in-law, Alexander, pull on their coats or vests. She smiled.

# CHAPTER 3

"Is there a maid able to attend the young lady?" Albert asked the clerk as they checked in to the Hoffman House hotel midday.

Miss Thompson was in a lobby chair, her eyes barely open, with Mr. Clawson beside her. They'd left the *Maybelle* without event and with no sign of the rough-clothed man or the well-dressed one, but he was not comfortable, feeling the hair on the back of his neck rise every time the doorman reached for the long brass handle of the hotel double doors, fully expecting some attack. He was shaken, he admitted. He'd never been involved with any subterfuge, least of all any dangerous-type maneuvers. But he felt as if he was in the middle of one now.

He'd been the subject of a rather sour look from the hotel clerk when he requested two of the three rooms have an adjoining door.

"We're not that sort of hotel, sir, if you get my meaning," the clerk said.

He leaned forward, feeling his patience fray. "The young lady is a friend. I will not have you besmirch her name. She is under my protection, and there is nothing untoward about it," he growled.

"Of course, sir," the clerk said and handed him the keys. "There are no maids available to help your *friend*. I'm very sorry. Most of the female staff are gone by now."

"Very well."

Albert took a long look around the lobby as he walked toward Mr. Clawson and Miss Thompson, nearly empty at this time of the day, although there were a few couples dressed in fancy clothing, heading to a restaurant or the theater according to the clerk's comments. Nothing seemed out of the ordinary, but then, what did he know about ordinary? He was rarely good at noticing the details of his surroundings, hence his hiring of Clawson, as he was usually absorbed in whatever medical treatise he'd recently read.

Thankfully, the Hoffman House hotel had a lift to convey them to the sixth floor; he was in no mood to climb that many flights of steps. Mr. Clawson took his key when they arrived at their rooms, and Albert waited for the bellman to light the lamps in Miss Thompson's room and pull down the blankets. He unlocked the door between the rooms and did the same in the other room. Albert tipped the man and carried his satchel into the other room after locking her door to the hallway. Miss Thompson stood silently and very still, leaning against a desk near the washroom. He cleared his throat.

"I have gotten us adjoining rooms just in case there is some t-trouble tonight, which I highly doubt as we were very careful making our way here. I'm leaving the k-key to the door between our rooms with you. Lock it once I am on the other side. I don't believe anyone got much s-sleep last night, and I intend to crawl into bed even though it is very early in the evening," he said and looked away, thinking about what he must ask her next. "Will you be able to d-d-disrobe without h-help?"

"Oh," she said and reached over her shoulders to the buttons there. "I can easily touch the ones at the top and at the bottom near my waist, but I won't be able to reach the ones in the middle." She looked up at him, her lashes wafting as she did, and whispered, "Perhaps you could undo those."

He swallowed and thought of the last time he'd attended an autopsy and the smell that had permeated his nose for days. Perhaps if he concentrated on that foul odor, he wouldn't be overcome with the scent of *her*. But there was nothing wrong about what he was going to do next.

Nothing dirty or shameful. He was helping a friend after two long, uncomfortable, and dangerous days. That was all. But when she gave him her back, her hands on the arch of the desk chair, her shoulders hunched forward, and he lifted his shaking fingers to the delicate ivory buttons, he stopped breathing, couldn't draw in air. As he undid each one, he exposed a very white, very female undergarment of some kind below a glimpse of pale, smooth back. His knuckles grazed her bared skin as he undid the next button, and he heard her sharp intake of breath. Albert glanced up, his heart pounding, and saw the two of them in the mirror over the desk at the same time she did, his hands at work on the back of dress, her lips parted, as if they were lovers.

He had no idea how long they stood staring at the intimate tableau.

"I'm sure I can manage the rest," she whispered.

He dropped his hands and stepped back.

"I think I will leave it on for now. I'm tired, but I think I may want to sit up for a short while. There is a book of poetry on the desk I will glance at. It has been quite a day," she said, turning quickly and removing the view that would undoubtedly torment him while reaching her hand behind her back to close the gap of her dress.

"Wait." Albert hurried to his room, digging through his bag for the flannel robe he always took with him when traveling. He turned back to her room, his hand outstretched. "Here. Use this while you sit and relax. It's clean."

She took the robe from him and smiled. "This looks like

something you've been wearing forever. I have a similar one in my room back home . . ." she faltered. "You did send the message I wrote to my family?"

He nodded. "As soon as we arrived. Don't forget to l-lock the connecting door after me," he said and checked her door to the hallway. "Good night."


KIRSTY PULLED OFF HER DRESS AND TOOK IT TO THE washroom. She patted a stain on the skirts with a wet towel and then washed her face, hands, and arms. She was exhausted but felt sticky and dirty from the long hours of travel and terror. She slipped her arms into the worn flannel robe of Mr. Watson's, pulling it tight over her chemise. The garment was huge, dragging on the floor behind her, but it felt like the only comfortable thing that had happened to her all day. It smelled like soap and like him. She curled up on the bed on top of the blankets and opened the book of poems.

But, similar to her experience the night before on the *Maybelle*, she woke with a start as the handle to her room from the hallway began to shake. She jumped from the bed, quickly picking up the key to Mr. Watson's room from her nightstand, holding up the robe, and running to the adjoining room's door. The key shook in her hand as she tried to get it in the keyhole, glancing back at the door to the hallway and hearing the unmistakable sound of a key rattling. She hurried through the doorway, closed the door, and turned the key in the keyhole.

"Mr. Watson," she whispered as she hurried to the bed. "Mr. Watson!"

He turned over in a hurry, sitting up and throwing back the covers. "Miss Thompson! Whatever are you doing in here?"

"The knob to my room turned, and I heard a key jiggling!"

He stood quickly and went to the adjoining door, his ear flat to the wood. Kirsty could not stop staring at him, at his long arms, roped with muscle, and his bare chest, dusted with dark hair that tapered to the waistband of a pair of loose pants that sat low on his hips. How could she have ever thought he was a physical weakling? The vision of his body made her warm all over.

He glanced at her and went to his bag sitting near the bed, pulled a shirt from inside, and slipped it over his head. She stood there, clutching his robe, bereft of the vision of him but staring anyway.

"How have they found us?" she whispered.

"Maybe it is hotel staff," he said softly.

Kirsty doubted it. Why would a maid sneak into a hotel room in the middle of the night? She watched as Mr. Watson went to the door in his room leading to the hallway, taking a deep breath before turning the knob.

"What are you doing?" she cried.

"Lock this door behind me."

"How will you get away from them! They will hurt you!"

He ignored her and opened the hallway door, stepped out of the room, and pulled the door shut behind him. She ran to the door and opened it a crack. Mr. Watson was speaking to another man who was wearing a wrinkled suit and a smashed hat with a key in his hands.

"That key says number eighty-eight. This door is number eighty-six," Mr. Watson said.

"Oh! Right you are! What a pickle! No wonder the dang key wouldn't work."

The wrinkled-suit man lurched down the hallway as Mr. Watson turned back to the room, eyeing her as she spied on him.

"What were you thinking?" he said as he locked the door to the room. "I told you to lock the door!"

"When you are furious with me, you don't stutter."

He stared at her and shook his head. "You walk right into danger without a thought to safety. Yes, I'm furious."

"Well, it did end up that it was just a mistaken hotel guest—drunk, I would guess," she said.

"Was it? I could not detect the smell of alcohol on that man."

"Oh!"

"'Oh' is right, Miss Thompson!"

"There is no reason to snap at me, sir. I didn't, after all, go out in the hallway with you."

"But you would have, I suspect, if whoever was crouched behind the potted plant by the elevator decided to make his presence known!"

"Of course, I would have if I had seen him," she said, as angry at him now as he was with her. "It would have been two against one, and you wouldn't have been able to defend yourself!"

"The point of all this subterfuge, however, is to keep you away from these men. You are the target. Not me."

She stepped toward him. "But you would have been hurt."

"And you would have been s-safe." His shoulders dropped on an expelled breath.

Kirsty inched closer and put her hand on him, feeling his warm, heaving chest through thin linen. "You are very heroic."

He looked up as if trying to determine what he would do or say next. His hand crept up and covered hers. He took a deep breath. "I am not heroic at all."

"Neither am I. I do not want to go back in that room by myself, Mr. Watson."

"You won't have to. Go c-climb into m . . . the b-bed. You are staying r-right here."

Kirsty glanced at the bed and then at his hand holding hers over his pounding heart.

"Where will you sleep?" she whispered.

"I'll be f-fine."

"Will you?"

He nodded and stared into her eyes. *This is what Lucinda feels like when James looks at her the way he does, what Elspeth feels when*

*Alexander touches her.* This gnawing yearning for a man in the pit of her stomach and lower. She stood on her tiptoes and kissed his jaw, feeling his whiskers against her lips, the smell of him, not unlike that wonderful flannel robe, wrapped around her, and she closed her eyes, reveling in the rightness of him.

Albert turned his head, a fraction of a movement. Her lips were at the corner of his mouth, and he could no longer control his actions with his superior brain and disciplined mental habits. His desire for her overwhelmed every intellectual ability he possessed. He turned a hair farther and touched his lips to hers, feeling himself completed. Ridiculous thought notwithstanding, it was true. He moved his hands to her waist, lifting her and pulling her against his chest. The feel of her breasts against him through the silk of her chemise, full and soft, made him draw a shaky breath. She sighed against his mouth, bringing her hands to the back of his neck, tickling him when she ran her fingers through the long hair there.

He wanted her. He wanted her under him in that bed behind them. He slanted his shaking mouth over hers and kissed her fully, his tongue touching her lips with a tentative stroke. She touched her tongue to his, and that was what broke him, hurried him forward, until her back was against the wall. He pressed his hips into hers, and she could surely feel the evidence of his desire against her belly. She opened her eyes and smiled, touching her tongue to her top lip. *My God, she is a seductress I cannot resist.*

"Mr. Watson," she whispered with a girlish giggle. "You have such a large . . . foot."

She would be a playful, wonderful lover. There would be no shame or recriminations in her bed, only sensual touches and laughter. Even being as virginal as she no doubt was. *She is a virgin.* And that thought was like a bucket of ice-cold water dumped over his head. He dropped her to her feet and backed up, running a hand through his hair.

"Miss Thompson, I b-beg your forgiveness. I've t-taken advantage of you in the worst way," he said, difficult as it was as she stared at his crotch, tented with his erection.

"You cannot take advantage of a willing participant, can you, Mr. Watson?"

He just stared at her, his robe hanging open on her, revealing a deep cleavage between her breasts. He turned then, hurrying to the bed and retrieving a pillow, which he threw on the floor at the foot of the bed. He stretched out on the carpet and rolled on his side, purposefully closing his eyes tightly. But he could hear her. He heard as she shrugged off his robe and held off a groan as she laid it over top of him, her smell enveloping him. He heard as she climbed into his bed, puffing the pillow and letting out a small sigh. He doubted he could sleep a wink.

MUIREALL THOMPSON WOKE WITH A START FROM WHERE SHE'D been dozing in the parlor of the Thompson home at 75 Locust Street, Philadelphia. "Has anything happened?"

"Nothing," James said. His wife, Lucinda, was upstairs in one of the beds trying to sleep, although he doubted she would. Nothing had happened as of *yet*, he thought, but James was sick with fear that the men after their family, especially after his younger brother, had taken Kirsty just like they'd taken Elspeth two years ago to hold her for ransom. There but by the grace of God she'd been rescued before anyone had harmed her more than could be healed. And in the end, Elspeth, always quiet and seemingly fragile, had killed a man with a knife as he beat her with his fists. He glanced at her as she came through the door.

"Mrs. McClintok is making some sweet rolls for us, and I've got tea," Elspeth said as she carried the tea tray awkwardly on her swollen belly. Her husband, Alexander, jumped to his feet.

"Let me carry that," he said. "You should be off of your feet."

Tears rolled down her cheeks. "I can't, Alexander! I can't sit still for one more minute worrying about Kirsty. I have to *do* something!"

"It's after four in the morning, Elspeth," James said. "We don't need tea."

"I'll have tea," Muireall said. "Where is Payden?"

"In the kitchen with Mrs. McClintok and Robbie, sound asleep on his arms at the table. I tried to get him to go to his room, but he will not listen to me," Elspeth said as her lip trembled.

"Elspeth, darling," Alexander led her to the settee, "please sit. You are upsetting yourself."

She looked at him and wobbled a smile. "I am being silly, am I not? But I just can't help myself."

"Is this what I have to look forward to?" James asked.

Muireall arched a brow, and their great-aunt Murdoch's eyes flew open. "What are you saying, boy?"

He shook his head and returned to peering out between the curtains to the street. "Someone is coming."

Alexander jumped to his feet and followed James to the front door. "Could you see who it was?" he asked.

"It looked like one of those telegram messengers," James said.

The brass door knocker clattered, and James pulled the door open quickly, yanked the man inside, and shoved him against the wall.

"Hey," the man yelled, losing his cap. "Whatcha doing? Leave me be!"

"Where is she?" James growled and tightened his hold on the man's neck.

"Don't know what you're talking about! Just delivering a message to 75 Locust Street!"

"Let him talk, James," Alexander said and held up the cap he'd picked up from the floor. "It says 'Bernardo's Messenger Service' on this card on his hat."

James released the man and stepped back. "What are you doing here? Who sent you?"

The man grabbed his cap from Alexander. "I'm here because my boss paid me extra to deliver the message in my satchel in the middle of the night. Special delivery from New York City." He looked up with wide eyes at Alexander, who was aiming a pistol at him.

"Slowly," Alexander said. "Pull out that message slowly."

"Here," the man said and handed over the recognizable telegram envelope to James.

"He might be telling the truth." Alexander lowered his weapon. Muireall slipped into the entranceway, coins in her hand.

"Here is a tip for your trouble."

"Don't want no money, ma'am. Just want to get out of here."

James opened the door, and the man ran down the steps, glancing over his shoulder as he did. James handed Muireall the letter. "It's addressed to you."

Muireall took the telegram and went into the parlor. She slit the envelope and pulled out two pieces of paper. She unfolded one and plopped down on the seat behind her, her hand over her mouth.

"What is it?" Elspeth asked. "Tell us!"

"She's fine."

Elspeth burst into tears, and James dropped down to his haunches in front of Aunt Murdoch. "Where is she?" he asked.

Muireall scanned the letter. "In New York. At a hotel. With Albert Watson."

"Albert? What is she doing with Albert?" Alexander asked.

Muireall began to read:

*Couldn't get off the boat. I am fine, with Mr. Watson in NYC hotel, someone tried to kill me, be home soon.*

"A New York hotel? I'm going to kill her," James said. "I'm going to f—"

"James," Lucinda said from the doorway.

"And then I'm going to kill Watson!" James said.

Muireall held up her hand:

*Miss Thompson safe but not out of danger. Escorting her home on the 16th.*

"He is the one that took her into dinner on the night of your party, isn't he, Alexander?" Muireall asked.

"He is, and although this is highly unusual, Albert is to be trusted. He'll guard Kirsty with his life if necessary."

"What could possibly be the reason she got on a boat?" Elspeth asked.

Lucinda walked into the room and sat down on the arm of Aunt Murdoch's chair. "I believe I know. She told me she wants to visit Scotland to meet the people she's been corresponding with about importing wool. She knows that Mr. Watson travels back and forth to England because he still has family there and for his work in medical research. She was going to ask him to escort her and a companion on a voyage to Scotland since he would be traveling there anyway."

"That is absurd! Albert would never agree to escort her," Alexander said.

"But it does sound so much like our dear Kirsty," Elspeth said and patted her eyes.

"How did she know what ship he would be on?" Muireall asked.

"That is my fault," Lucinda said. "My aunt's stepson has been meeting with Mr. Watson and getting help from him with some advanced studies. Kirsty was at our house the day Geoffrey told us of Mr. Watson's plans to sail on the *Maybelle* on the fourteenth."

"Good God, that girl will be the death of me," Aunt Murdoch

said. "And she's going to have to marry this Watson person after this escapade."

"We must not jump to conclusions, Aunt," Muireall said.

"Be realistic, Muireall. Kirsty, our Kirsty, sleeping in a room alone with a handsome man—and I think he was, if I remember correctly. She'd be . . . energetic," Aunt said.

Alexander looked away, and James gritted his teeth.

"If he has touched her, I'll kill him, regardless of how *energetic* she was," James growled.

"I fear this is my fault." Lucinda turned to Muireall. "Of course, I discouraged her plans before that day with Geoffrey, but I never in my wildest dreams thought she would board the *Maybelle*."

"Kirsty can be . . . unpredictable, Lucinda. You could not have prevented this."

"Also, energetic," James said and shook his head. "I'm going to kill her."

Payden McTavish Thompson, the Tenth Earl of Taviston, moved from the door where he'd been standing, listening to the telegrams Muireall read. "But more than any of it, they are back. Plowman is back, and we must be on our guard."

# CHAPTER 4

Albert pulled Miss Thompson through the crowd at the train station, his arm around her shoulders. Clyde was on his other side and glanced up at Albert with a furious look as he bent down and pinned a ladies' hat to his hair. From the back, Albert hoped it would look like his assistant was Miss Thompson and the dark wig she now wore would confuse the men following them. The hotel clerk had purchased their tickets ahead of time so he would not have to stand in line at the ticket house, and Albert had summoned a hat maker who carried a wide variety of wigs. They had arrived at the station very close to the train's departure. The whistle blew, and the crowd surged forward.

Albert maneuvered Miss Thompson to the steps of the car directly ahead of them and stayed close behind her as they walked down the aisle, looking for two open seats. Clyde went to a different train car and would keep the hat on until the train left the station and their seven-hour trip began. Miss Thompson seated herself in a window seat, and he sat beside her on the aisle. He watched passengers board and find seats, looking for a flicker of interest in his companion. The second whistle blew, and he could hear the conductor shouting in the next car to squeeze together on the benches there. He'd paid extra for first-class tickets and had been told to board car number fifty-six to find seats with padding instead of a wooden bench.

"I've got to take the wig off. It is so very hot. Have you seen anyone suspicious?"

He shook his head. "I haven't."

"I am so tired," she said. "I didn't sleep well at all."

He hadn't slept well, or at all, on the floor, reliving that kiss between them for most of the night. He was certainly no lothario, as he was mostly too distracted by his studies and work to find a woman to have relations with, whether just for a night or for longer even, but that did not mean he didn't have a sexual appetite. He did. He just didn't indulge it all that often, and the few times he found a woman willing to indulge it with, the experience was often disappointing.

He did his duty by his mother by regularly dining with her and whichever woman she was hoping to pair him with, although he never took the next step. Never met up with the young lady in the churchyard after escorting his mother to services. Or asked if she'd enjoy sharing a coffee some afternoon or visiting the park. He just never did any of it. But this woman beside him . . . this was different, and even with poorly developed social skills, he recognized that he wanted to see Kirsty Thompson again. Maybe every day. Maybe forever.

She yawned widely beside him and scrunched down in her seat. It was not long before her head was leaning against his arm and she was breathing deeply, even with the noise of the tracks and the chatter of the crowded car. He wanted to gather her up in his arms, kiss her forehead, and tell her she was safe to drowse, that he would watch over her. He fought sleep until he could no longer keep his eyes open. He woke with the side of his face resting on top of her head and smelling whatever soap she used on her hair.

"Are you awake now, Mr. Watson?"

He sat up quickly and ran a hand over his eyes. "I'm so sorry. I fell asleep."

"No need to be sorry," she said and glanced up at him through thick auburn lashes. "Perhaps you did not sleep well last night either."

"I d-did not," he said and looked down into her face, her head still nestled against his shoulder, just inches away. They stared at each other for a few long moments until her focus settled on his mouth.

Something dropped onto his lap, and she sat up quickly. "That was Mr. Clawson who just walked by, I think."

"Yes," he said and opened the folded paper laying on his leg.

*Bad actors in the car behind you. Watch your back, sir.*

"How does he know? Did he see any of them yesterday? I don't think he did," she said, straining to look over her shoulder.

"Miss Thompson, please turn around. I don't want them to notice you if they are coming."

"Oh yes," she said and promptly turned back. She smiled up at him. "You are so clever."

He stared at her as she looked out the window, humming a low tune and tightening her gloves. "Thank you."

She turned back to him, wide-eyed. "I wish I had a knife."

"Excuse me?"

"A knife, Mr. Watson. Muireall gave Elspeth a knife before she went to the Pendergast ball, and she hid it in a little pocket on the side seam of her dress. She stabbed a man and killed him."

"You look particularly cheerful about that, Miss Thompson."

"Oh, I am. I wish I'd been there to stick a knife in his eye while she stabbed him in the stomach, where Muireall had told her to."

"A bit bloodthirsty?"

She shook her head. "No. Anyone who attacks our family will face consequences."

There was no shading her view of the world. No gray area in her morality or her heart. There was right and there was wrong, and her decisions did not appear to lay heavy on her conscience. He let himself think about the aftermath if he had to pull out the pistol laying in the bag at his feet and wondered how it would feel to take a life or injure another person. Would he feel guilty? He thought he might. Kirsty Thompson, however, would have no second thoughts.

"Whatever are we to do if they confront us here on the train?" Kirsty whispered.

"I highly doubt they will. And Mr. Clawson has settled himself on the bench just ahead. And as you mentioned, Mr. Clawson did not see any of your attackers, only having the descriptions we gave him, so perhaps he is mistaken."

She smiled up at him and thought about how much better she felt hearing his sensible words and conclusions. But then it occurred to her. "Mr. Watson, you are not stuttering anymore."

He swallowed and turned his head, facing front. "Just so."

"What does that mean, 'just so'?" she asked, more than a little exasperated.

"It means I d-do . . . do not wish to discuss it."

"Oh." She stared out the train window, watching the fields and trees go by. "But sometimes when we talk about something that bothers us, it can make us feel better."

The passing landscape was hypnotic, but Kirsty was not sleepy. She wanted to be alert in case Plowman's men showed their faces, and she wanted to know more about Albert Watson. She wanted to know what sort of activity he did to make his chest so muscular and his stomach so flat. How wonderfully it narrowed to lean hips barely holding up his drawstring drawers. But what was more vivid in her mind's eye was his face as he'd kissed her, the way he'd stared at her mouth, and that moment when he'd seemed to lose all control and pushed her against the door letting her feel the length of him against her belly. She groaned.

"Miss Thompson?"

"I—I didn't eat much yesterday. I'm just hungry, Mr. Watson. I'll be fine."

"I imagine we'll be making a stop at the next station long enough for passengers to buy something from the vendors just before we reach Trenton proper. And also to use the, um, the facilities."

"I'll definitely need to use the facilities," she said cheerfully and noticed his blush. "Don't care to use the hopper closet unless absolutely necessary."

"I will purchase food for us and have Mr. Clawson escort you to where you need to go."

"When will you get to use the necessary? I don't imagine trains wait long at the stations, do they?"

His face reddened. "We should not be discussing such a thing. It is too improper to be mentioned."

"Too improper to let go of your water? My brother James just says 'take a piss,' but Muireall gets very angry when he says that."

"Miss Thompson, please!"

"Or you could go to the last train car and go in the breeze," she said with a laugh. "Women, of course, cannot do such a thing with skirts and petticoats and long drawers. Men are so lucky!"

He was looking at her as if she'd lost her mind, and he was bright red in the face. He turned away from her and stared straight ahead. He turned back to her once, opened his mouth to speak, stopped, and looked forward again. He certainly was prickly.

"I am not accustomed to d-discussing such subjects with gently raised young ladies. Or with anyone," he said finally.

"Earthy matters, you mean, Mr. Watson? Aunt Murdoch has

often despaired of my tendency to say what is on my mind without regard to my audience. I see now that I have offended you. I'm very sorry. Let's talk about something else. Tell me about the speeches you give when you speak to other doctors, although I will admit I didn't quite understand everything you said when I heard you speak at the University of Pennsylvania."

"On that occasion, I was discussing the work we are doing on the sources of fevers and infections, I believe. Rather boring stuff for a young miss as yourself to waste away an afternoon."

Kirsty thought about watching Mr. Watson as he spoke to his audience that day at the university auditorium, how hushed and enthralled they had been, and how commanding and brilliant he sounded. She could have listened to him all day, to his deep voice, and looked at him too, at the curl of his hair that fell over his forehead and at his long fingers pointing to something on the large charts he had on stage beside him. He was nothing like the men she'd envisioned she'd be partial to, nothing at all.

"It was not a waste, Mr. Watson," she said softly and looked out the window. "Not a waste at all."

THE TRAIN SLOWED, AND AS ALBERT ESCORTED MISS THOMPSON down the steps that had been lowered by the conductor, he spotted Clawson waiting for them. He told him of his plans and glanced back at the passengers still descending the steps. Miss Thompson laid a hand on Clawson's arm with a smile, making his assistant blush. She had not blinked an eye at Clawson's scar. He was indebted to her for that. The young man had been horribly burned trying to rescue a younger sister from a fire in their home, and Albert had been one of the doctors seeing to his recovery and later to his separation from the opium that had been used to numb the severe pain from his burns. Albert had spent many evenings reading to the young man from books from the library at the university on every subject imaginable. He'd hired Clawson as soon as his scars and pain were manageable. He'd been thinking of hiring a secretary anyway, and his salary allowed for it, and even if it had not, he was not a poor man.

His own father had been a doctor of renown in London, treating dukes and earls and marquesses, and even members of the royal family on occasion, and had been amply rewarded. Wendell Watson had provided well for his widow and had passed the bulk of his estate to his only son. They had moved to America over ten years ago when his father had accepted a position at the Harvard Medical School, although he only lived to teach for two years there, succumbing to a heart seizure during a lecture he was giving.

The intrigue, danger, and the damsel, to be whimsical about his current affairs, were nearly more than his orderly mind could process, although he understood he must stay on his guard and be willing to do whatever was necessary to keep Miss Thompson safe. He paid for ham sandwiches wrapped in paper and bottles of root beer soda, still fizzing after the round man behind the counter had popped off the caps, scanning the crowd all the while for his charges.

"Are you ready to board, Miss Thompson?" he asked when she made her way to him on Clawson's arm. He looked over their heads, trying to see if anyone was following them, but it was too crowded to tell.

"I am. Give me those sandwiches. Carry the bottles, Mr. Clawson. Hurry now, Mr. Watson. You can have a few minutes alone while we board and take our seats." She turned away from him, sandwiches in hand, and nodding at Clawson, who'd taken the bottles from him.

"Thank you." He hurried to find a gentleman's room in the station.

He climbed the steps on the train car as the second whistle

blew and was barely in his seat when they lurched forward. Miss Thompson was nibbling at her sandwich but had not touched her root beer. "Is root beer not to your taste?"

"Oh no. I love it," she said as she glanced at the bottle. "I just don't know how many other stops we will make."

He chuckled. "It seems we are unable to hold any conversation without referencing an . . . unmentionable."

She laughed and leaned toward him, smiling and mischievous. "Earthy, sir. We refer to them as earthy."

She was the most beautiful woman he'd ever seen. She was beguiling and drew him closer to her with every moment spent in her company. He smiled at her, regrets already building, as she would choose a husband from a wide swath of Philadelphia society, especially with her connection to the Pendergasts, and it would not be him. Him? What on earth made him think about being a husband? Her husband, of course.

The long ride through New Jersey toward Philadelphia was done quietly as Miss Thompson looked out the window, her hands folded in her lap, humming a tune he heard from her occasionally. He was soon engrossed in a medical article written by Joseph Lister on the subject of cleaning surgical instruments and the dramatic decrease of deaths after surgery.

He lifted his head when that lovely young lady beside him pinched his hand enough to leave a bruise. "Ouch!"

"I have been trying to get your attention, Mr. Watson," she said in a breathy voice, her eyes darting the length of the train car. "I think the man who was drunk in the hallway of the hotel just walked past us."

"Are you certain?"

"Not completely, but I'm fairly sure. He is wearing a minister's collar today."

"We are not far from Philadelphia. We will depart the station as quickly as possible and hire a carriage to take you home."

She looked at him then, her face wreathed in worry. "We will be no match for them, I'm afraid."

"I intend to guard you, Miss Thompson. I will not let anyone harm you. I promise."

She shuddered a breath and laid her head on his shoulder. "I've been imagining what would have happened if you hadn't found me on the *Maybelle*."

"Do not make yourself uneasy. And there is no use dreaming of tragic endings. We are closer to your family with every turn of the train's wheels, and then you will be safe. In the interim, I will have to do as your protector. Mr. Clawson and I."

"I feel so much better when you talk sensibly to me," she whispered and clutched his arm. "You will come into the house with me? Explain what has happened?"

"Your family will be so glad to have you back in their arms, any anger will be short-lived. And I wouldn't want to impose on a family reunion."

She harrumphed. "Short-lived? You do not know my family."

The train was on time, a near miracle in Albert's estimation, when they rolled into the Philadelphia station. They had not been delayed by broken tracks or a herd of pigs or any other obstacle that so often made train travel less than timely. Miss Thompson was still leaning against his arm, although she was not sleeping, and had long ago slipped her hand into his. He'd spent much of the last hour looking at one of the marvels of the human body, the hand, and observing the differences between his and hers. Those twenty-seven individual bones, allowing humans to grip and fist and caress, were dainty and dwarfed by his. He rubbed his thumb over her knuckle as its tendons and muscles tightened, bending her finger against his with soft pressure.

As the train slowed into the station, Clawson took his bag, as they had discussed, intending to go directly to the home Albert shared with his mother to deposit his belongings and check to see if his trunks had been delivered. He would have both hands and the gun in his pocket to protect Miss Thompson until he could hand her over to the safekeeping of her relatives. The train chugged to a stop and he stood, offering his hand to her to rise, guiding her to step in front of him. He kept his hand on her shoulder as they slowly walked down the aisle, waiting to depart the train onto the crowded platform. He bent down and looked out a window and saw Clawson, who nodded and turned into the crowd.

Albert took her hand as she stepped down and slipped his arm around her shoulders, keeping her tight against him as they moved toward the street, away from the house that served as the train station, now a tavern and inn. There were carriages for hire, and he quickly hailed one and gave the address to the driver. He glanced over his shoulder as he helped her climb in and saw two men heading their way that could have been the hotel drunk and the man behind the planter, one wearing the collar of the church.

"Make haste, please," he said to the driver. "There'll be extra for you if you get us moving immediately."

Albert was not quite in his seat when the carriage driver maneuvered out of the line of carriages and into the street, weaving in and out of slower vehicles, and causing him to drop hastily down next to Miss Thompson. He risked a glance back and saw no one following.

"They were there, weren't they?" she whispered, tightening her grip on his hand.

"They were, but we are on our way now. Everything will be fine."

"But you don't know that."

"Your family will keep you safe," he said and squeezed her hand.

She was silent for a long moment, staring out at the passing businesses, turning back to him with wide eyes and a trembling lip.

"What is it, Miss Thompson?"

"I prefer you, Mr. Watson. I prefer you to keep me safe."

He stared at her, willing himself not to gather her in his arms and kiss her. And then she turned away from him and pointed as the carriage slowed down. He stepped down quickly, helped her alight, and reached to pay the driver and ask him to wait to see him home as well. As he turned, a fist connected with his chin.

# CHAPTER 5

"James! What are you doing?" Kirsty shouted and pulled at her brother's arm. "Stop it!"

"Get in the house, Kirsty! I will handle this." James grabbed Mr. Watson by the collar. "I'm going to kill you if anything has happened to my sister!"

"James," Muireall shouted and turned to her. "Get in the house, Kirsty."

Elspeth hurried to her, ungainly in her haste, hugging her and swaying. Kirsty felt tears gather but was determined to stay calm, even feeling her heart pounding in her ears with the knowledge that she was home, home at last. She heard a grunt behind her.

"James! Stop hitting Mr. Watson! Stop it! You will hurt him!"

"That's my intent, girl. I have some things to say to him!"

Suddenly, James stopped. "James," Lucinda said calmly, "we must not make a spectacle for our neighbors. Come into the house. Kirsty is safe, as you can see."

"Mr. Watson, you must come in for some ice for your eye," Kirsty heard Elspeth say as Muireall hurried her up the steps, James close behind. She would thank her sister later as she had no desire to allow Mr. Watson to leave quite yet.

She went into the parlor with Muireall, and Aunt Murdoch hugged her and held her face in her hands. "You've done it now, girl," she said in a shaky whisper as James began shouting again.

"I am so angry; I don't know what to do with myself! Do you have any idea how worried your sisters and brother and aunt have been? Do you? You hie off without regard to anyone else, to the danger you've put yourself in, that you've put the whole family in!"

Muireall shook her head. "What were you thinking, Kirsty?"

"Not thinking at all!" James said.

Kirsty could feel every eye on her and even those purposefully looking away. She would not cry. She would not! And then Mr. Watson was beside her, holding a towel to his eye.

"I think that's enough shouting at the young lady," he said in his measured voice. "Miss Thompson had a significant fright. Allow her to recover herself, and I'm sure she will explain all."

James angled himself to Mr. Watson, hands on his hips. "You're here to tell me what to do in my own home? How I'll address my sister, who I'm responsible for! You stupid bastard."

Alexander caught his arm. "James. She is safe. Elspeth is crying. Please take a breath. We were all terrified. You as well."

James backed away, his eyes still on Mr. Watson's face, she noticed as she glanced at him because she'd been staring at him too. How perfectly wonderful to have this man defend her, even though she was well able to handle anyone in her family, including James, who had a hot temper when he was emotional. Mr. Watson was staring back at her, and she smiled.

Lucinda reached her hand through Mr. Watson's arm. "Won't you please sit over here near the window so I have the best light to examine your eye?" she said.

"Thank you. First, I would like to put this weapon in a safe place," he said as he drew the pistol from his pocket.

"Give it to me, Albert," Alexander said. "I'll store it until you leave."

"Tell us, Kirsty" Elspeth said. "From the beginning."

And so she did, eliciting an angry response from Muireall when she told them how she'd boarded the ship and could not get off. "And then we were walking down a narrow walkway when someone tried to shove me in the water. There was no railing, just a length of chain. Mr. Watson caught me just as I felt my feet leave the deck." She swallowed, feeling the terror anew. Elspeth was holding her hand and glanced over her shoulder to where Mr. Watson sat.

"I didn't realize at first that someone had pushed me on purpose, but Mr. Watson was certain there were two men working in conjunction. We went to his stateroom," she continued and heard a growl from James, "and waited there until it was time to get off in New York. Mr. Clawson got us our meals and brought them back to our rooms."

"So you were in the sleeping room with *two* men," James hissed.

"How wicked you make it sound," she said angrily. "It was not. They saved my life!"

"Who is Clawson?" Elspeth asked.

"He is Mr. Watson's assistant. He is the one who took care of canceling all of their plans." She looked down at her folded hands. "They were to travel on to London, as Mr. Watson was giving a speech there, but he canceled his appointments to bring me here," she whispered.

"I heard you were to travel on to England, Mr. Watson," Lucinda asked him.

"I was to speak at the Royal Academy, but Miss Thompson found herself in need of an escort."

"Thank you, Albert," Alexander said. "We're indebted to you."

"And you went from the ship to the hotel?" Lucinda asked.

Kirsty nodded. "He got a room for each of us, and mine had a connecting door to his, which he made me lock and keep the key. The hallway doorknob on my room rattled in the middle of the night and woke me. I went to his room and, foolish man, he went out into the hallway and confronted the man trying to get into my room. Although that man was acting drunk, Mr. Watson said he was not. I was terrified, Elspeth! Just look at him! He would be no match in a fight. And then he was furious that I had not locked myself inside as he'd told me to do. I kissed him then, and he made a bed on the floor, and I slept in his bed because I wasn't going back into my room alone."

After that had come pouring out of her mouth, Kirsty looked up into Elspeth's wide eyes. When she looked around the room, she noticed James looking as though he'd just eaten nails, Lucinda and Aunt Murdoch were smiling, and Muireall was her normal unreadable self. She glanced over her shoulder and saw Mr. Watson rise from his chair, his face a brilliant red color.

"Mr. Thompson, Miss Thompson," he said with a nod to James and Muireall. "Might I have a w-word?"

Kirsty watched the three of them leave the room and looked at Elspeth. "What could that be about?"

"He's going to offer for you, girl," Aunt Murdoch said. "Still a gentleman, even though he's an Englishman."

"What? What are you talking about?"

Elspeth took her hands and held them tightly. She waited until Kirsty looked at her and then smiled softly. "He's going to ask you to marry him, dear."

Kirsty jumped from her seat. "Oh no! He cannot do that!"

Alexander stepped in her way as she hurried to the door.

"You will not allow Albert to be honorable?"

"Honorable? What are you talking about, Alexander? What does honor have to do with this! We hardly know each other."

"You were alone with him for two days. You slept in his hotel room bed. He kissed you," Alexander said softly.

"But nothing more happened! I'm certain you kissed Elspeth before you married her!"

"She was my intended."

"That is not fair! He is brilliant and does important work and will be famous one day! Why would he care to marry me?" She stole around her brother-in-law and went directly into Muireall's small office when she heard voices from within. "What is going on here?" she demanded.

"Mr. Watson has asked our permission to marry you," Muireall said.

"Asked you?" Kirsty said to her sister. She turned her glare on Albert Watson and poked him in the chest. "I am not a child, and this is not the Middle Ages. I will decide on my own whom I will marry when I am asked!"

There was barely room to turn around to make a suitable exit in Muireall's small office, Kirsty thought with some annoyance. Then Mr. Watson laid his hand on the edge of the desk and dropped to one knee, forcing James to squeeze behind Muireall's chair.

"Miss Thompson, would you do me the g-great honor of being my wife?"

"Oh! Oh! Mr. Watson! They are forcing you to say this, I'm sure."

He shook his head and reached for her hand. "No one is f-forcing me to do anything. I'm asking for myself."

"But why? Why would you want to marry me?"

"Christ, Kirsty," James growled. "The man's on his knee."

Mr. Watson cleared his throat. "I-I am enamored w-with you, Miss Thompson. You are beautiful and l-lively and extremely clever. I c-can offer you comfort, security, and some travel if you wish. I b-believe we will suit w-we . . . fine, if you will have—"

"James! James!" Kirsty heard from the hallway.

James pushed his way past Mr. Watson, still on his knee, and wrenched open the door. "Lucinda! Dear Lord! What is it?"

"It's Elspeth! It's her time!"

"I'll go for the doctor," he said and headed for the front door at a run. "I'll be back as soon as I am able!"

Mr. Watson stood and quickly went out the door and into the

parlor. He knelt at Elspeth's side. "Mrs. Pendergast. Can you tell me how long it is between your pains?"

Elspeth shook her head as she took short breaths, her hand resting on her stomach. Her husband was white-faced staring at her, his hand resting on her hair.

"I would say seven or eight minutes," Aunt Murdoch said and glanced at the watch on a chain at her waist. "I was watching her face. She was trying to hide the pain, but I could see it."

He rose. "Mr. Pendergast, please help your wife to one of the bedrooms. Miss Thompson, is there a nightgown of someone's she could wear? I will need spare sheets and hot water, a very sharp knife that has been boiled, and thick thread that has been boiled as well."

"Mr. Watson," Kirsty said. "You are not a doctor, are you? Do you know anything about delivering babies? Perhaps we should wait for the doctor."

He turned to Alexander. "I've my medical degree, although it is not in obstetrics. I have never worked as a medical doctor, however, because I went directly into research after completing my internship at the hospital and therefor never used the honorific of doctor. I have delivered two babies on my own and assisted in several other births."

"Can you help her, Albert?" Alexander whispered as Elspeth groaned.

"Yes. I can help her. Let us get her upstairs and comfortable."

"But you are hurt yourself, Mr. Watson! James pummeled you!"

He turned his head to Kirsty. "I was able to withstand the violence, Miss Thompson, as you see. And Mrs. Thompson has put ice on my eye, so there should be little swelling."

IT WAS JUST AS WELL THAT ALBERT DID NOT HAVE A FRAGILE OR overlarge ego—medical school beat it out of a man fairly quickly —but even still, it would be gratifying if his almost fiancé would quit acting as if he were weak or unable to protect himself. He would have been murdered anyway, but he purposefully had not returned James Thompson's blows. This was her brother who she loved dearly and who she probably thought of as a father figure. He wasn't going to engage in fisticuffs with him on the street. She would resent him for it—eventually. And he found he did not wish to hurt her or lose her good opinion.

He followed Alexander up the steps slowly as the father-to-be was holding his wife to his side and she had to stop several times to catch her breath and once to allow herself to let the pain of a contraction subside. He checked his watch and did not believe this would be a protracted birth, nor would he be surprised if this child appeared within the day.

The eldest sister and the aunt stood at the top of the steps.

"Your old room is ready, Elspeth," Muireall Thompson said. "Aunt Murdoch and I will help you get changed and comfortable. Come, dearest."

"I suspect this will be a quick birth, Alexander," he said to his friend, who was now staring at the closed door of a bedroom. "Your wife's pains are coming closer together with each one."

"She said to me this morning that her back was hurting her terribly. I should have made her go home then." He turned to Albert with stricken eyes. "If anything happens to her . . ."

"You must not think like that. She is going to need you in the hours and days to come, so you must keep your wits about you and remember you are not the first man to stand outside of a birthing room."

The door opened, and the sister came out. Albert went in and closed the door. The great-aunt with the rheumy eyes and the quivering hands stood by the bed. "I helped deliver this girl and her siblings when it was their time to enter the world. I intend to be here when this young one arrives. If it is your wish to have me leave, then you must carry me out."

"I am happy to have experienced staff at my side, Mrs.

Murdoch," he said as he washed his hands with the thick soap beside the basin.

"You'd better call me Aunt Murdoch, boy, seeing as you're going to be part of this family in the not far ahead future."

Albert sat in the chair beside the bed while the aunt stood at the window and occasionally wiped her neice's brow with a damp cloth. There was nothing to be done for some time, he suspected. He chatted about mundane subjects to the mother-to-be, helping her breathe through the pain of the contractions, and checking his pocket watch as they became closer and closer.

He stood at the side of the bed, checked Mrs. Pendergast's pulse, and felt her extended abdomen. He looked down at the patient and smiled. "I believe you will be delivering a son or daughter very soon. When the pains come, feel free to scream or cry. I'm going to examine you now. Do you understand?"

"Yes," she said and blew out a breath. "I wish . . . I wish Alexander were here."

"There's no place for a man in a birthing room," Aunt Murdoch said. But Albert had already opened the door to the bedroom.

"What? Has something happened already?" Alexander said as he clamored to his feet from where he sat in the hallway.

"Your wife would like you to be with her."

Alexander's face went completely white, and he swallowed visibly. "I wouldn't want to be in the way."

"She has asked for you, and it is not as if you will be called on to be in any pain," he whispered.

Albert closed the door behind Alexander and instructed him to wash his hands and pull a chair near his wife's side. "She is going to squeeze your hand as the pains come and you are going to help her push when I tell her to."

Albert laid a sheet over Mrs. Pendergast's knees and began his examination. He called the aunt to his side. "She is crowning.

We're going to begin very soon. Is the knife and thread here and boiled?"

"Mrs. McClintok brought them up the back stairs while Elspeth was climbing. They were in a rolling boil for five minutes."

"Excellent." He raised his head over the sheet to the patient's face and smiled. "On the next contraction, I'm going to ask you to push, Mrs. Pendergast. Alexander, support her back."

And so began the most wondrous and miraculous action of the human body, a woman's human body—the birth of a child.

Albert stood, child in his arms, and looked up at the parents. "Congratulations. You have a fine, healthy son."

Mrs. Pendergast smiled broadly and reached out her arms to him. Her husband slumped in his chair, one arm behind his wife's back and one wiping the tears from his face. Aunt Murdoch hurried to a knock at the door.

"Ah, come in, Dr. Maxwell." She then stuck her head out the door to those waiting in the hallway. "We've a new Thompson! Elspeth has been delivered of a healthy baby boy. She is fine; however, Alexander will need smelling salts soon!"

KIRSTY STARED AT MR. WATSON THROUGH THE OPEN DOOR AS he wiped his hands on a towel Aunt Murdoch had given him. He'd removed his coat and his sleeves were rolled up, revealing long muscular forearms with hair a shade or two lighter than the dark hair on his head. The sight of him speaking to Dr. Maxwell stirred her—his words and demeanor were confident, she could tell, even though she didn't understand some of what he said. He was in his element speaking with other learned men about subjects she'd no understanding of and looked so very handsome. He smiled at Elspeth when she asked him something, and Kirsty's heart fluttered.

"What is happening?" James said as ran up the steps. "Elspeth! Is Elspeth all right?"

Lucinda stepped in front of him and held his arms. "She is fine, James. Mr. Watson delivered her of a healthy baby boy just a few minutes ago. Dr. Maxwell is speaking with Mr. Watson about the birth right now."

James's shoulders dropped. "Watson delivered this child?"

The bedroom door opened, and Alexander stepped into the hallway holding the newborn, staring down into his son's face. "We're going to name him Jonathon. I had a brother who died of an illness when he was very small, and we've decided to remember him this way. Jonathon James." He looked up at James, his face tearstained. "She wants him named for you too, James. You mean the world to her."

James looked up at Alexander, and Kirsty thought she saw her brother's lip tremble before he turned and hurried down the steps. "I'll see Elspeth when the women are done their fussing," he said in a husky voice over his shoulder. His wife smiled and followed him sedately down the steps.

"What can I do, Alexander?" Kirsty asked him as he wiped his face with shaking fingers. She noticed Mr. Watson slip out of the room, still talking to Dr. Maxwell.

"Sit with Elspeth while I go downstairs and send a message to my parents and to Mrs. MacAvoy at the house so she can have everything ready when we get home." He looked at her keenly. "I was privileged to be there, you know. It was a wonder. And your sister . . . your sister is so strong . . . so brave. She was in so much pain!"

She kissed Alexander's cheek and lifted Jonathon from his arms. "Go. Go tell your parents. They are worried, I'm sure. I'll sit with Elspeth."

Alexander hurried down the steps after telling Elspeth he would be right back and to not go anywhere while he was gone. Kirsty walked into the room and sat down on the chair beside the bed while Aunt Murdoch and Mrs. McClintok gathered up bloody sheets and toweling, laughing with the other women about Alexander's comments. As if the new mother could climb out of bed and run away! Muireall was helping Elspeth wash her face and arms and put on a clean nightgown. Elspeth was chattering and crying and laughing.

"I'm so exhausted," she said finally. "I'm washed and on clean sheets and think I will take a nap."

Muireall helped her lie back and then turned to Kirsty, taking the child from her arms. "I remember when Payden was this small." She smiled wistfully. "So very precious and fortunate to have such wonderful parents. Our Elspeth will be a very good mother, and you know Alexander is besotted with her and will be so with all of their children. Wait until they have a girl!"

Kirsty laughed with her sister, picturing their stoic brother-in-law with tearstained cheeks. She sobered and looked up at Muireall. "I'm sorry. Truly, I'm sorry about getting on the *Maybelle* yesterday. I wasn't thinking, as you have rightfully pointed out, and have brought danger to us again. You're well within your rights to be furious with me."

"We were only angry because we were so frightened, you know. We are well aware that sometimes you are carried away on a whim," she said softly and rocked side to side as she held the child. "What are you going to do about Mr. Watson?"

"About what?"

Muireall eyed her. "About sleeping in the same room with him. About kissing him. About his marriage proposal."

"It seems as though he has forgotten about it, and I don't intend to bring it up. Everyone was in such turmoil over Elspeth . . ." she trailed off as there was a knock at the door.

Mr. Watson stood in the hallway. "Dr. Maxwell is going to stay for a bit and check on your sister before leaving. May I s-speak to you a moment before I go?"

She glanced back at Muireall, who raised one eyebrow, and headed down the stairs, Mr. Watson following her.

"I thought we m-might speak outside where it is not q-quite so crowded."

James stepped into the foyer as they came down the steps. He shoved his hands in his pockets as Lucinda looped an arm through his. "I suppose I owe you an apology for hitting you, especially now after you tended Elspeth."

Mr. Watson smiled. "None necessary, Mr. Thompson."

"Actually, the words are necessary, and he has yet to say them," Lucinda said, smiling up at Mr. Watson.

James growled. "I'm sorry. I shouldn't have hit you, but she's—"

"That's enough, James," Lucinda said and pulled him back toward the parlor.

"Come along," she said to Mr. Watson. She stared down the quiet street, happy to feel the breeze in her face but wondering if they should venture past their stoop when she heard James call her name.

"I've got a friend watching the house, and Alexander's family's security man will be sending patrols. You can walk down the street without danger, Kirsty," he said and turned back into the house.

Mr. Watson stared at her. "This d-danger is significant. I hadn't quite thought clearly about what you'd t-told me. It was your sister Elspeth who was kidnapped."

She nodded. "Did you notice the scars on her wrists? They've not faded, and I'm not sure they ever will."

## CHAPTER 6

Albert was finally alone with her, and his tongue was tied. She didn't want to marry him, if her declaration during his interview with her brother and sister were any indication, although he knew she was not immune to him. That kiss had convinced him of that.

"Miss Thompson, h-have you considered my p-proposal?"

"You should not allow my family to harass or pressure you."

"I've not allowed them to p-pressure me; however, I consider your r-reputation and my honor allow only one solution. M-Marriage."

She began to walk the tree-lined street, her hands behind her back. "Sometimes others' expectations serve to remind us of the behavior we should all strive for," she said and turned her head to look at him. "And sometimes those same expectations are utter garbage."

He stared at her. It was easy for one to think that Miss Kirsty Thompson was a beautiful, flighty, empty-headed young woman. In fact, it was possible that some of her behavior encouraged that belief. But clearly she was much more than that. She was loyal to her family in a way that did not feel natural to him, as his mother and he did not have a warm relationship, nor did he have one with his only other relative in America, his cousin Fredrick. While her brother James and sister Muireall were open about their anger with her, she was not afraid to be angry right back, having no fear that she would lose their love, as it was clear they loved each other, even the in-laws. What would that be like?

"You're right, of course. B-But I cannot like the idea that someone would s-sully your reputation. You were caught up in a dastardly p-plot that makes me wary of every leaf that moves on this street."

"Did you mean any of it?" she said softly after a few moments.

"Pardon?"

"Did you mean it? What you said in Muireall's office."

She was looking straight ahead; he could barely hear her words and could not see her face at all for the brim of her bonnet. And for as bold as she could be, she was unsure of herself. It was reassuring to him, in a way, that she had doubts, as he did. "Do you mean when I said I am enamored w-with you? That you are beautiful and l-lively and so very clever?"

"Yes, that."

He thought he detected a tremble in her voice. "I d-did. I meant it all."

She stopped walking and turned to him. "I've always hoped to be in love with my husband and he with me. I don't remember too much of my parents. I was only five when they passed, but even to my young eyes, I could see that they loved each other, and everything I've been told about them confirms that. Alexander and Elspeth adore each other, it is clear. James and Lucinda love each other just as much, although both are less obvious in their feelings. I want the same, Mr. Watson. But I don't love you, and enamored is not love, even if it is flattering."

"Perhaps we should t-take our time, then. Perhaps I could court you and see how we feel after a longer period of time."

She smiled the smile that always shook him to the soles of his shoes. It lit her beautiful blue eyes, highlighted the few freckles across her nose, and made him focus on that mouth of hers, the one that he wanted to kiss every moment he was near her.

"I would agree to that, Mr. Watson. Maybe we will come to have deeper feelings. I will admit I enjoyed our time together, not considering the danger, of course. You are so brilliant," she whispered. "It is hard to imagine a man such as yourself being interested in me."

"I-I am interested."

She tilted her head. "Why is it, Mr. Watson, that you stutter when you are talking to me, but when you are talking about medical issues or to Elspeth and Alexander, you do not stutter at all?"

He could feel his face turning red, glanced away and back at her face. "It would be hi-highly inappropriate for me to d-discuss it with you."

"But why?"

"Because, Miss T-Thompson, it has to do with something . . . something *earthy*, that I should n-never discuss with you."

"You've aroused my curiosity, Mr. Watson. I should—"

"Kirsty," they heard and turned to Muireall standing on the stoop of their home. "Mr. and Mrs. Pendergast are here. Perhaps you would like to greet them."

"Coming, Muireall."

"I'll be on my way then," Albert said.

"You must come in and say good-bye, Mr. Watson. You cannot get away from us so easily."

He followed her back to her house, shook hands with Dr. Maxwell as he left, and went into the sitting room, a cozy room with a fireplace and an alcove with book-filled shelves and a comfortable leather chair beside a window. At the other two tall windows, where he'd been seated by James's wife so she could examine his eye, there was a cluster of chairs and a large quilting hoop. It was easy to envision this family spending much of their time here in one another's company. He was greeted enthusiastically as the hero on his current entrance into this room, unlike when he'd arrived earlier directly from the train station.

Alexander was pouring whiskey for the men, and Mrs. McClintok was passing out glasses of wine for the ladies and spoke over the chatter of the family assembled. "I'll have luncheon out on the table in the dining room in a few minutes, everyone," she said and turned quickly, hurrying through the door. "Oh dear, the cake is due to come out of the oven this very minute."

"Payden? Robbie? Help Mrs. McClintok in the kitchen, please," Muriel said.

"I'll check on the table and make sure there are enough place settings," Kirsty said and looked around. "You are staying, aren't you, Mr. and Mrs. Pendergast? And you, Mr. Watson?"

He'd eaten little and was hungry and knew his house would be in an uproar if he requested a meal outside of the designated times set by his mother. He nodded and followed her into the dining room. "We'll need two more chairs," she said and dragged one from against the wall, squeezing it in between the others and doing the same on the other side of the table. "Open the long drawer in the hutch behind you, please. We'll need forks, dessert forks, knives, spoons, and napkins."

"There are several kinds of forks," he said.

"Yes, there are, Mr. Watson. There are salad forks and oyster forks, but the ones with the longer tines, the dinner forks and the dessert forks, are all we'll use." She stopped her arranging to stare at him. "Have you never set a table before?"

He shook his head and picked up several of the forks from their velvet-lined compartments in the long drawer, looking for the ones with the longest tines. She was soon at his side showing him the differences between the cutlery. She handed him the silverware, lifted an embroidered napkin from beside the separate compartments, and turned to the table. "Over here, Mr. Watson.

This is where I've added a place for you beside me, and we'll put the Pendergasts beside Alexander."

She picked up a tray then and instructed him to distribute a glass to each place setting. It occurred to him that he would have no idea where the forks and glassware and linen came from at his home. There were servants; there had always been servants to attend to all those details, and his mother, of course, would have it no other way, still living as if it mattered that her husband had been given a baronetcy for his service to the Crown and that she was Lady Althea Watson. What would his mother have to say about Kirsty Thompson?

He looked up then as Kirsty's chattering and laughing family came through the open window-paned doors to the dining room at the same time Payden Thompson and another young man, Robbie McClintok, the housekeeper's son, he guessed, came though the swinging door that led to the kitchens, carrying platters of relishes and pickles and baskets with steaming hot rolls and a large dish of butter.

"I've put your parents beside you, Alexander. How is Elspeth? Will she be hungry?" she asked her brother-in-law.

"I just checked." He took a shaky breath and smiled. "She and Jonathon are sleeping."

The eldest Miss Thompson sat at the head of the table and Mrs. Murdoch at the foot. Everyone else seemed to know exactly where to sit and did so as Mrs. McClintok wheeled in a cart with a massive painted urn and a stack of plates that resembled flattened soup bowls beside it. She stood still beside the cart, her son at her side, as Muireall Thompson bowed her head and the rest of the diners followed suit.

"Dear Lord, we thank thee for all of your blessings and especially for the newest member of our family, Jonathon James, and for his parents, Alexander and Elspeth, too. We are thankful that Kirsty arrived home safely and that Mr. Watson was here to help young Jonathon on his journey from your hands into our world.

We thank you for the roof over our heads and the food on our table. In Jesus's name, amen."

Albert looked around the table as the others raised their heads and Mrs. McClintok began to dip a thick, steaming stew into each dish. Her son carefully took them from her and served them, beginning with the great-aunt and the eldest daughter. He saw the younger boy, Payden, take a glance around the table and snatch a roll, dropping his hand to his lap.

"Payden, we will begin to eat when everyone is served. Put that roll on your bread plate," the eldest sister said. Kirsty chuckled beside him.

"I didn't get much of a breakfast as everyone had to fuss over Elspeth," he said.

James pointed at the boy with his fork—his dinner fork. "We don't whine at this table, young man, and your sister was deserving of every bit of attention she received."

He put the roll back in the basket. James's wife was seated beside Albert. She leaned close. "You will grow accustomed to meals at the Thompson house, but it does take some time."

"It is quite relaxed."

She tilted her head. "That is one word for it."

The stew was delicious, and Albert found himself wiping the bowl with his third roll, as he'd seen James do. His mother would have called it peasant fare, but he could not get enough of it, as well as the chatter around their dinner table. There were multiple conversations going on from one end of the table to the other and laughter, constant laughter. It made him feel morose about the meals he shared with his mother and often his cousin Frederick. The quiet, dull, and dutiful courses that marked the meals served at their home, Charter House.

. . .

"It looks as though you like Mrs. McClintok's cooking." Kirsty smiled as she watched him clean the bottom of his bowl with the last bite of roll.

"It's all delicious."

She stood and motioned to her brother, and Mr. Watson jumped to his feet, as did the rest of the men at the table. "Come, Payden. We'll clear the table and carry in the coffee and cake so Mrs. McClintok and Robbie can eat their dinner while it is hot."

She gathered empty plates and followed Robbie and Payden into the kitchens. Mr. Watson came through the swinging kitchen door rather awkwardly, holding the butter dish and the roll basket.

"Where shall I put these?"

"Anywhere, Mr. Watson," Mrs. McClintok said as she wiped her mouth with her napkin. She was eating at the big, scarred kitchen table and motioned Robbie to sit down across from her. "The coffee and tea are both ready, Miss Thompson. They're on the back of the stove with a towel over them to keep them warm. Just put them on the tray there with the cups and the cream."

Kirsty readied the coffee tray and handed Payden the cake plates to carry. "Can you get the cake, Mr. Watson?"

He picked it up gingerly and held it as if it would jump out of his hands. He glanced at the door swinging back toward them after Payden had gone through.

"I'll hold the door," she said, caught it as it swung inward, and held it open against her back. He was staring at the cake as he passed her, concentrating on his task. He was adorable in his consternation, if a man well over six feet in height could be adorable. For all his confidence and knowledge while delivering a baby, and most likely on whatever task he set himself to, Albert Watson was not comfortable doing the most mundane things. James would have carried the coffee tray and the cake and maneuvered the door with little problem. But this man was not a Thompson.

He placed the cake in front of Muireall, as she'd asked him to, and held her chair while she sat the tray down in front of her and poured coffee and tea for her family. She was on the last cup when they all turned to a commotion in the hallway. And then they heard MacAvoy shouting.

"Elspeth! My God! How is Elspeth?"

A door above opened, and soon they heard Aunt Murdoch, who had gone to check on the new mother. "She is sleeping, you giant oaf! Quiet!"

Moments later, MacAvoy came barreling into the dining room and skidded to a stop. "Tell me she and the bairn are well."

Alexander and James jumped from their seats, rushing to MacAvoy, both grinning and all three laughing with even a few self-conscious hugs between them as they shared their happy news.

"Are you hungry, MacAvoy? There is chicken stew and chocolate cake," Muireall said. I'm sure the stew is still hot."

"That sounds delicious," he said, nodding to Muireall and the Pendergasts. "I'm just done at the factory and will need to wash my hands. I ran out of the house as soon as Eleanor told me the news."

"Why didn't you bring her?" Kirsty asked.

"She wouldn't come. Said there was too much to do to get the house and staff ready for Mrs. Pendergast and the new babe," he replied as he walked to her and kissed her cheek, whispering in her ear. "Thank God you are safe. James sent me a note when he received yours from New York." Then his eyes trailed to Mr. Watson. "And who is this gentleman?"

MacAvoy stared at Mr. Watson as he pushed his chair back and stood, turning to MacAvoy as he did, the two men nearly equal in height. He extended his hand. "Albert Watson."

"MacAvoy."

"It's a pleasure, Mr. MacAvoy."

"It's just MacAvoy, and it's no pleasure."

"Mr. Watson delivered Elspeth and Alexander's son, MacAvoy," Muireall said.

"Did he now?" MacAvoy said. "And when will you be offering for our Kirsty, you being a *gentleman* and all?"

"There is no reason for anyone offering for my hand!" Kirsty said, but the room had already erupted. She glanced at Mrs. Pendergast, who was wide-eyed, her hands covering her smiling face.

"I can't wait to tell Annabelle! She will be so excited! Albert is such a dear man!"

"Mother," Alexander began.

"Mrs. Pendergast? Let me—"

The room quieted when Mr. Watson spoke. "Thank you for your kind words, Mrs. Pendergast. But it would be premature to speak about any nuptials or even partiality. Miss Thompson has agreed, however, for me to escort her to an event at the college where I lecture. I'm hoping she'll agree to further outings in the future."

Kirsty smiled at the Pendergasts and turned to MacAvoy. "Here. Sit at my place. I'll get you your plate," she said and then whispered, "and then I will dump it in your lap."

James followed her into the kitchen. "Don't blame MacAvoy. That was probably my fault."

"What exactly did you tell him?" Kirsty asked as she dipped the stew into a bowl and picked up two rolls. "I was not going to tell Annabelle anything about it."

"Why not? She's your best friend."

"Because she told me not to go to the *Maybelle*. That something bad was bound to happen," she said, feeling her face redden.

"Well, she was right."

"She was," Kirsty said softly and looked away. "Is it necessary for you to repeat my failures, my ineptitude, James? I understand what I did was foolish. I am regretful and have repeatedly said I am sorry. Is it really necessary to make me feel worse than I do?"

She had not realized that Mr. Watson had come into the kitchen and was standing nearby, and neither did James, she thought. Mr. Watson took the bowl from her hands and smiled.

"Allow me, Miss Thompson. Won't you come back into the dining room? You've yet to finish your cake."

She looked up at his handsome and serene face. There was nothing judgmental to be found in his eyes or his smile. In fact, there was only warmth and encouragement.

"Of course."

Mr. Watson insisted she take his seat and finish her tea before he spoke to Muireall and James. "Miss Thompson, Mr. Thompson, I want to thank you for allowing me to dine with you this day. I told Dr. Maxwell I would check on your sister before leaving, which I will do and then be on my way. It was good to see you Alexander, and you as well, Mr. and Mrs. Pendergast. Mrs. Thompson," he said with a nod. "Please give my thanks to Mrs. McClintok for a fine meal."

Kirsty waited until she heard steps coming back down the staircase and went to the foyer. She was holding his hat. "How is she?"

"She is fine. There is always a danger of excessive bleeding for new mothers, but I've seen no evidence of that here. Mrs. Murdoch has assured me that someone will stay the night in her room with her, as I have recommended she not travel to her home until tomorrow at the earliest."

"We can never thank you enough, Mr. Watson. Elspeth is precious to us."

"I was glad I could be of assistance. I've asked Robbie—I think he's the housekeeper's son, if I'm not mistaken—to find a carriage for rent for me, and I believe it is w-waiting outside, Miss Thompson."

She looked up at him. "It has been quite an adventure."

He smiled at her. "I'm unaccustomed to k-kidnappers, delivering babies, or dinner with such an . . . enthusiastic family. But truly, I w-would n-not change a thing," he said, and she watched his Adam's apple bob. "If not for all of that adventure, I would n-not have had an opportunity to g-get to know you, Miss Thompson, and therefore I cannot r-regret any of the other."

"Oh," she said, feeling the shimmer of tears in her eyes. "You are so sweet to me."

"You are w-well worthy of k-kindness," he said and harrumphed a laugh. "Especially as it l-looks like you'll be joining me for a lecture on b-bone structure at the college."

She took his hand in hers and squeezed it. "I very much look forward to it."

He huffed a breath, looking elsewhere until finally bringing his eyes back to hers. "I am very g-glad of it. Good day."

# CHAPTER 7

"Whatever has happened, Albert?" his mother asked when he found her in her favorite chintz-covered chair in the room she called the drawing room. "That *Clawson* person said you were not going to London! Have you contacted your Uncle Bertrand? Louisa will be expecting you! You must send a transatlantic immediately, even though it will be quite expensive. Albert? Have you heard what I've said to you?"

"Yes, Mother. I've heard it all. C-clawson has already sent a telegram to Uncle Bertrand and Aunt Louisa with my apologies."

"Whatever happened? *Clawson* was quite mysterious and would not give me any answers! And I do not understand why that person must live here! In our home!"

"We have the space as there are sixteen bedrooms in this house aside from the staff quarters. It isn't unusual in England for a s-secretary to live with his employer, and it is convenient for me to have him here. And he does have his own entrance."

"It is bad enough that you have him dine with us occasionally. I would have insisted on his own entrance if he did not! I don't want to be seeing him coming and going at all hours.

"And Graybell and Mrs. Munchin live here in their own apartments."

"Of course they do! B-butlers and housekeepers always live with their employers."

"And often so do secretaries."

She opened the magazine she was holding. "As usual, you are determined to ignore my wishes."

He'd only been marginally aware of his mother's histrionics until after his father died. He was away at preparatory school and then college, and when he was home, he spent most of his time reading medical books and working with his father while he was alive. It had come as rather a shock that his mother was as unpleasant as she was, which he'd discovered after his father's funeral. From what he'd been able to wheedle from Graybell over the last few years, his mother's behavior had not changed. It had just been hidden from him. He loved her. She was his mother. But he often wondered how a wife would ever fit in.

"A friend needed an escort, and I provided it, and therefore I did not sail with the *Maybelle* to England. Mr. Clawson will reschedule my speaking engagement, and I will ask Aunt Louisa if it will be c-convenient for us to stay on a new date."

"Of course it will be convenient! Whyever would they not want you to stay with them? Your father was a successful and well-regarded physician to the highest echelons of British society and Bertrand just a merchant."

*Just a merchant*, Albert thought to himself. Uncle Bertrand had made a fortune in bits for horses, although his wide range of metal products included everything from rails for the ever-expanding British railroads to containers for flour and sugar. "I'll just want to make sure they have not made plans to travel or entertain other guests. I wouldn't want to be a burden."

"Don't be ridiculous. They don't travel. Louisa is a spendthrift, and they've three daughters to launch, none of whom show much promise to be beauties." She looked at him with panicked eyes.

"Whatever you do, do not let yourself be caught in a compromising position with the two eldest. Louisa would love to see one of them married to you and moved here to America, to live in my home!"

"Calm yourself, Mother. I've no intention of marrying any of my cousins."

She took a deep breath, her back straight, her hands clenching a handkerchief, and turned her head to look out the front windows. "I've been preparing myself for your marriage. You'll need to have sons to carry on your father's title. I will have much to teach a young woman about household management."

The reality of his situation came crashing down on him at that moment. His mother, *his mother*, could make it nearly impossible for him to have any sort of normal relationship with a woman. Although in his last letter, Uncle Bertrand had replied to his subtle questions about how his father had managed his mother's tendency to drama through all the years of their marriage with this advice: *Stand firm. Your father never raised his voice and did not allow your mother's moods to threaten his, for as you know, my brother was the most even-tempered and pleasant person one could ever meet! What else he did not allow was when she disparaged another person, especially staff. I know you love her, as any dutiful son should, but your mother can be cruel, especially, it seems, to those of her sex.*

"I will see you at dinner, Mother," he said, refusing to begin a conversation about who actually ran the household—his mother or Mrs. Munchin.

"Where is Mr. Watson taking you?" Muireall asked.

"To the College of Medicine. There is a speaker tonight he wanted to hear, and then there is a reception for the speaker."

"I'm more than happy to go with you," Muireall said from where she leaned against the door of Kirsty's bedroom.

"Please don't," Kirsty said and blew out a long breath. "I didn't mean that to come out quite that way. It's just that James is insisting on taking me in his carriage, and then I will be inside with Mr. Watson and a roomful of very smart men and women. Oh dear, I don't want to make a fool of myself, but I am old enough to spend a few hours with a man unchaperoned."

"You will not make a fool of yourself. You are a Thompson. And James is escorting you there because he is concerned about Plowman."

Muireall directed Kirsty to sit while she pinned her hair up in a fashionable style and fixed a small hat with a flower made of green silk ribbons to the very top of her head. "Oh! That looks very nice," Kirsty said at last. "I did want to look my best."

Muireall stepped back as Kirsty stood, shaking out her skirts as she did. "You will never have to worry on that score, dear. You are a beautiful, if occasionally impetuous, young lady. Elspeth and I have often bemoaned the fact that you received all the good looks from our mother. You are a picture of her, I imagine, as she looked when she first married Father. Aunt Murdoch says it's true too. She says sometimes it takes her a moment to remember that you are Kirsty and not Cullodena."

"I wish I could still see her in my mind's eye. I can't any longer, haven't been able to for years. I look at their portrait, but they are just painted subjects, not real any longer in my mind."

"But they are in your heart, Kirsty. They always will be."

They heard James's voice as he climbed the steps. "Come on, girl! You don't want to be late, do you?"

"Coming," she said and stopped to kiss her sister's cheek. "I don't ever want to disappoint you, and yet I know I have. What would we have done without you all of these years?"

"You would have done just fine. I was just the oldest child. Nothing special. Just the oldest."

"You took care of us all."

"Kirsty! Are you coming?" they heard from the foyer and smiled at each other.

James rode with her in his new carriage, alternately complaining that he now owned a carriage when he had two very serviceable legs and instructing her on what to do if Albert Watson took liberties.

"Alexander vouches for Mr. Watson, James, and you trust Alexander."

"I do, but I don't trust any men with my sisters."

Kirsty laughed. "What will you do when you have daughters! You'll be threatening young men every day if any of those daughters are as beautiful and self-assured as Lucinda."

James smiled. "She is a beautiful, brilliant woman, and she picked me."

She supposed that was what she wanted from a man. Her brother was proudful of many things, and his arrogance had been his downfall on some occasions. But his looks, his build, his successes in the boxing ring were none more important to him than the fact that Lucinda Vermeal had chosen him to marry.

They pulled up in front of the University of Pennsylvania's College of Medicine and saw Albert Watson waiting on the steps. He walked toward them when Kirsty waved.

"Here. Take this," James said to her as Mr. Watson wound his way through the crowd. He handed her a sheathed dagger, its covering heavy leather that had been carved in an intricate design.

She shook her head. "No. You are being ridiculous. Mr. Watson would never abuse me in such a way that I would need to stab him," she said with a nervous laugh.

"It's not for Watson. It's for Plowman's men."

She looked up at him with wide eyes, his staring back at her. There was nothing charming or humorous or even irritated about James Thompson's gaze at that moment.

"Take it," he said. "Do you have a pocket in that skirt?"

"Yes, yes I do," she said and quickly took it from him, pushing it into the pocket hidden in the folds of her skirt. She looked up as Mr. Watson approached.

"Good evening, Miss Thompson, Mr. Thompson," he said and looked directly at her. "Are you ready to step down?"

"Yes. Oh yes." She reached for his outstretched hand. James kissed her cheek as she moved past him out of the carriage.

"Watson," James said. "If I am not here in this carriage on this block at ten this evening, take my sister somewhere safe and then get word to the family when you can. I'm trusting you to keep her unharmed if the worst should happen."

"I don't see something dreadful happening here inside our new medical school, Cohen Hall—"

James cut him off. "I'm trusting you to guard my sister. You must trust that I have a better understanding of the dangers to our family. Elspeth was taken from us in the middle of a fancy party at Alexander's parents' mansion. I don't take any chances."

"Of course. I'll do whatever is necessary if your carriage is not on this block at ten."

"Enjoy yourself, Kirsty," James said as looked at her. "And don't forget what I've told you."

Kirsty watched the carriage roll away and then took Mr. Watson's arm. "I've been very much looking forward to this evening, but I am nervous too. All these very clever people will know that I am not. Clever, that is."

"You're extremely bright, but I'm not sure how much you will enjoy this speech. I am very glad you agreed to come, though."

"I was very happy to get your note with the particulars for this evening. I thought perhaps you'd forgotten."

FORGET KIRSTY THOMPSON? NOT LIKELY. HE DID HAVE AN odd sense that there was some destiny at play that evening. But there was nothing odd about how right it felt to have Miss Thompson on his arm. She was looking particularly lovely and chattering up at him with a smile, her blue eyes twinkling. He escorted her into the hall and helped her be seated. She was looking all around her, smiling and nodding if she met someone's eye and taking in the beautiful architecture of the lecture hall. The crowd hushed and the lights lowered when the chairman of the medical school stepped onto the stage to introduce the evening's speaker.

Albert lost all track of time as he listened to the doctor on stage. Once he was brought quickly back to reality when Miss Thompson leaned up and whispered in his ear, her breath warm against his cheek. "I wish I'd brought pencil and paper. I would have liked to make some notes."

He looked at her with admiration, for she was not being coy. She was completely sincere and shushed him when he bent toward her to reply.

"I want to hear this part," she whispered, and he thought she was the most contradictive and darling woman he'd ever met.

She clapped enthusiastically when the speaker was done and asked several questions as they made their way to the reception area. She looked around at the assembled group of researchers, doctors, and other academics as if she'd found a new species.

"This is lovely, although the food table is a bit sparse," she said, and he laughed.

"It always is. Professors are generally strapped for funds, and doctors spend years building lucrative practices. They're generally terrified to spend a p-penny more than is absolutely necessary."

She smiled up at him, clinging to his arm. "Well, if you were the host, I would make certain there were plenty of tasty dishes and desserts so everyone would stay and enjoy themselves. Oh. There is Mr. Clawson. Mr. Clawson," she called out and waved at his secretary.

But he was still envisioning the picture she'd painted. The one where she was his hostess. He wanted this cheerful, beautiful, and clever woman in a way that frightened him. It was not the easily identifiable sexual need, although there definitely was that. There was more to it. There were quiet dinners and happy reunions after a day apart and gentle touches when the world was a dark place, as it was on occasion. He stared down at her, wishing they would never be parted and keenly aware of the longing in his chest.

"Look who is here, Mr. Watson! It's Mr. Clawson. How silly of me! Of course you know your own secretary."

Clawson was stuttering and swallowing and totally ill at ease as she threaded her arm through his and led him to the buffet table. "Are you coming, Mr. Watson?" she said gaily over her shoulder.

He followed behind the pair of them, she talking and laughing and poor Clawson nodding in time. He stopped when there was a hand on his shoulder. He turned to see his friends Caleb Brock and Gladys Clark.

"Ah, Caleb! Gladys! Dr. Benjamin was excellent, didn't you think?"

"Oh yes. A very good speaker," Caleb said.

Gladys glanced at the buffet table. "Who's the young lady, Albert? She's very pretty."

"Miss Thompson. Miss Kirsty Thompson is her name."

"Is she associated with one of the colleges?"

Albert shook his head and watched her walk back with Clawson.

"I have put enough on my plate for the both of us." she said with a laugh. "There seems to be a dish shortage." She turned to Caleb and Gladys. "Oh! Hello! Are you friends of Mr. Watson?"

He made the introductions and watched her charm his friends who, like most in academia, were closeted with their own kind and not familiar with her brand of enthusiasm or her outgoing nature. How proud he was to have her beside him!

"Import wool, you say?" Gladys asked.

"There's plenty of places for me to sell it. I've talked to shop owners and seamstresses, and they would love to offer their customers authentic Scottish wool and yarns. I have to get it here, though." She bit her lip. "I've ordering and shipping and storage details I've not worked out yet."

"But you will," he said.

She smiled up at him, and he felt as if were ten feet tall rather than just his six feet and three inches.

"I will," she said and looked at Gladys. "Are you a professor here too?"

Gladys shook her head. "No lady professors at Penn. I teach at the Philadelphia Female College."

"Oh. I'm not familiar with it. Tell me about it," Kirsty said, her eyes focused on Gladys.

She asked intelligent questions and was willing to say she didn't understand something. She'd clearly won both Gladys and Caleb's appreciation as they laughed with her over some comment she'd made. She was the perfect woman for him, he was certain, even though she was so beautiful and he was at best an average-looking man with an accursed stutter. She would be an incredible help to his career and be a lively. intelligent companion, as well as a bed partner . . . *a bed partner*. And for a few incredible seconds, he did not remember the existence of his mother and thought that marriage to Kirsty Thompson was possible.

"It's nearly ten, Miss Thompson. We should be getting outside," he said.

"Oh," she said, clearly disappointed. "I've enjoyed myself ever so much. It was nice to meet you both, and I imagine I will see you again sometime, Mr. Clawson. Oh dear. That was presumptuous of me, wasn't it?"

"N-not if I have anything to do with it," Albert said and turned to his friends. "It was good to see you both. Miss Thompson's brother will be waiting to take her home."

Gladys stopped her with a hand on her arm. "Some of the women at my college meet monthly for a meal and some fellowship. Would you like to join us, Miss Thompson?"

"I would love that," she said and glanced up at him. "Although I can't imagine what I'd be able to contribute, but I'd be glad to be included."

"I will send word through Albert," Gladys said.

He smiled down at Kirsty and pulled her arm through his, escorting her down the long hallway toward the entrance of the building. He reached around her to open the heavy windowed door, thinking about the lost opportunity for a good-night kiss, and heard her gasp. She was running down the steps of the college screaming her brother's name before he was able to get out the door. Then he saw what had caused her panic. Under a gas lamppost a block away, he saw James Thompson squaring off against a man. The crowd leaving the speech were pointing and wondering where the police were.

He took after her at full speed, catching up to her quickly since she had dainty shoes and yards of petticoats interfering as she ran.

"No! You must stay back!" he said as he caught her around the waist.

"Let me go!" she shouted. "James needs my help!"

"He does not need to worry about you, Miss Thompson." He turned her to face him, holding her by the shoulders. "He's a grown man and a fighter too."

"You are right, of course," she said and looked down at the ground.

"Your wish to help is commendable, but—" He dropped his hands from her arms, and as soon as he did, she was gone, running to her brother.

He ran after her, barely catching her as she aimed for the man facing her brother, a knife in her hand.

"I lost me whole week's pay at your last match!" the man shouted.

"Never should have bet against me," Thompson said, his hands at his sides—but ready. "I don't want to hurt you. Go on home."

Albert watched as Thompson turned and backed away from the horses, the man following him. "Get her inside the carriage," he said to Albert without looking away from the other man.

Albert turned to her. "Please, Miss Thompson. Your brother is well able to handle this person. Allow him, and myself, peace of mind, and step into the carriage. As you can see, even his driver did not step down to help his employer."

"My luck, I'd get in the way of that great bruiser's fist," the coachman said from his seat. "He don't need me to keep him safe."

"You're right, I suppose," she said. "Well. It doesn't seem as though I can manage one meeting with you without causing a scene of some sort. I'm sorry. I didn't mean to embarrass you in front of your colleagues."

"There's no need for an apology. You were rushing to defend your brother," he said and turned his head to see what had become of the standoff.

The man threw a punch, and James Thompson caught the fist in his hand, swinging the man around by it until he tumbled to the ground. James dug in his pockets, pulled out several coins, and put them in the man's outstretched hand, closing his fingers tightly around the money as the man shook his head, trying to clear his thoughts.

"Now go home. Feed your family and don't gamble unless you can afford to lose." He looked up at his sister and pointed. "The carriage."

She took Albert's hand and, on the first step of the carriage, leaned over to kiss his cheek. "Thank you, Mr. Watson. I had a lovely time this evening."

He stood staring as she settled herself in the seat, barely noticing her brother coming over to him.

"She is the most devious of all of us. Gets it from Murdoch, I've always thought," Thompson said to him. "She'll be a handful for any husband."

"Whomever would be fortunate enough to win your sister's hand would be a lucky man."

"I was under the impression you were courting her," Thompson said and stepped close, his back to the carriage, blocking any view his sister may have had. "There is still a matter of your escapades in New York, Watson."

"I'm well aware of my obligations. However, I would be prepared to allow her to say whatever she wanted about me to save her from a miserable existence as my wife."

"Miserable existence?"

Miss Thompson leaned out of the carriage. "What are you two talking about?"

"Nothing, Kirsty," Thompson said and pulled himself into the carriage.

Albert watched the carriage pull away from the street. He was quite certain that this particular conversation with James Thompson was not finished.

# CHAPTER 8

"Do you like Mr. Watson?" Elspeth asked. Kirsty was enjoying an afternoon with her sister and holding her nephew after he'd been fed and had his diaper changed. Elspeth settled herself in the rocker beside the crib and held up her arms for her son. "Let me see if he will go to sleep."

Kirsty kissed Jonathon's forehead and handed him to Elspeth as the door to the nursery opened. Alexander peeked around the corner.

"Is everything all right?" he whispered.

Elspeth smiled at him. "He's just eaten and can barely keep his eyes open."

"That's my boy." He smiled back at her. "Do you need anything?"

"We're fine, darling," Elspeth said. Her husband blew her a kiss and quietly closed the door.

"Is he always like this?" Kirsty asked.

Elspeth stared at her son with a soft smile. "He can hardly bear to be away from us. I'm sure his devotion raises some eyebrows, especially with the men in his family, as they are very focused on the mills and their other concerns, like James's sporting arena. But I couldn't be happier. I love him so desperately, and really how could I complain that he wants to hold his son and kiss my hair?"

Kirsty sat down on the floor, straightening her skirts over her legs and leaning back against the flowered chintz-upholstered chair. "Is that what it is like? Marriage, I mean?"

Elspeth shrugged, rocking slowly, Jonathon's fist clenched around her finger. "It's not always perfect; one only has to think about the men who've left their wives and children. We're extraordinarily lucky, Kirsty. Our family always had enough food on the table and warm clothes to wear, and Alexander's family's wealth is beyond anything I could imagine. We are very fortunate. But I can't help but hope that if Alexander were a coal miner that we would still be as devoted to each other. Still love each other as much even with the additional challenges that poverty might bring."

"I believe you would still love each other if you did not have all the luxuries we are accustomed to."

Elspeth looked up and smiled. "You still have not answered my question. Do you like Mr. Watson?"

"I do like him. I'm not sure it is love, but I do like him. So often I find myself thinking about him. About what he is doing or where he is or if he has remembered to eat, which is something I fear he would forget when he is caught up in his studies."

"He was wonderful when I had little Jonathon," Elspeth said. "I would have laughed out loud at his comments to Alexander, who was decidedly green in the face, if I hadn't been in such pain."

Kirsty laughed. "When Albert came out in the hallway to get Alexander, I thought the poor soul would faint. Every little bit of color that remained in his face drained away when Albert told him you'd asked for him."

"It's possible you'll end up married to him, you know," Elspeth whispered as she stood to lay the baby in the crib.

"You don't think Muireall and James will insist, do you? And even if they do, I don't believe I'd allow them to force me. Maybe a few years ago, but at twenty years old, it seems medieval, doesn't it?"

"No one will force you, but there will be gossip to contend with."

"Gossip? I don't understand why that has everyone so out of sorts. It's not like we run with any social set that cares about that sort of thing. I don't see Mrs. Mingo, our neighbor on Locust Street, commenting about my unmarried state."

"Of course not. But say you do meet someone you're interested in. It's likely Muireall or James or even Alexander will look into that person. Our family will want to make sure that the person is worthy of you, doesn't have any terrible history with women or money, and isn't dangerous."

"And you're saying this person—or his family—would look into me in the same way. They might find that I traveled to New York with a man who was not a relative and stayed in a hotel at his expense. Who paid for all of my meals and lodging."

Elspeth nodded. "Yes. That is what they might find. It's certainly possible that someone you know saw you board the *Maybelle*."

"It's all such nonsense," she said as she stood. She was certain she had seen someone who knew her but she was still holding out hope that she was not recognized. "Nothing happened."

"Nothing?"

"Well, he did kiss me, and I was in his robe," she said as she stared out the window. "It was glorious."

Her sister blushed. "The doctor has said Alexander and I may resume . . . relations next week. I am looking forward to it very much."

"I wanted to do all that there was to do." Kirsty turned from the window, shaking her head. "I hardly knew myself. I never thought those feelings could be so overwhelming."

"And it only gets more wonderful with time and practice." Elspeth whispered with a smile.

"Does it?"

"Oh yes. And it is such a strange thing if you think too much about it. I could never, ever imagine doing it with anyone other than Alexander. Could you kiss anyone as intimately as I think you kissed Mr. Watson?"

Kirsty thought about all the men who'd been attentive to her in that way. It certainly could not be Bertram at the butcher's, or John Williams, who she'd met at one of the Pendergasts' affairs. John was handsome and well-spoken, but she couldn't ever imagine having his tongue in her mouth. There were several gentlemen she'd met though Annabelle, Alexander's sister, but she was not at all interested in seeing any of them without their shirts, although she often thought about Mr. Watson in his drawstring pants that night in New York and, as she drifted off to sleep, contented herself with the vision of him as his head dipped to kiss her.

"No," she whispered. "Why is that?"

Elspeth smiled and wrapped her arm around her shoulders. "You will just have to puzzle it out, I think."

"I suppose I will."

"How did your luncheon go with Mr. Watson's friend? Muireall said you met her when Mr. Watson took you to the lecture at the college. She told me where you were when I stopped by Locust Street last week."

"Gladys Clark is her name. It was fine. I enjoy meeting new people, but I felt as if I'd traveled to another country and did not speak the same language, although it was all plain English."

Elspeth laughed. "Surely not!"

"No, not all of it, but when one of them would bring up a topic they were teaching, all I could do was listen. I certainly had nothing to contribute. They were all so intelligent! Just like Mr. Watson."

Elspeth frowned at her. "Surely you have not succumbed to the idea that if a woman is stunningly beautiful, she must have an empty head, have you?"

"I am not beautiful. I mean, I know I am not unattractive in my way, but I am no prettier than you or Muireall and surely not comparable to Lucinda, but then we always knew James would marry a beautiful woman."

"You *are* beautiful, Kirsty, in a way few can compare to; however, your face will never overshadow your kindness and your quick mind." Elspeth held up her hand to stop Kirsty from speaking. "You have a head for what people will buy, and I'm sure you'll display it in a way that tailors and shoppers will not be able to resist your goods. Just because those women were talking about a subject you were unfamiliar with does not mean that they are knowledgeable about what you are an expert in. You've been the reason we've been able to get Thompson canned goods into so many grocers. Even Muireall says so. And you know Muireall does not hand out compliments all that often."

"They did ask me all kinds of questions about my shop, what it would be like and where I would get my wools."

"Of course they did. You have been working on this project for years. Your perseverance is the reason you are so close to a victory. A woman business owner! There are not that many of you. I am so very proud of you, and I have told Alexander that when Jonathon is bit older I intend to offer my services at your shop a day or two a week—if you will have me."

Kirsty hugged her sister and kissed her cheek. "Have you? You silly goose! I was wondering if I'd be able to tear you away once in a while. You can bring Jonathon with you if the weather is fine."

"We'll make it a family affair, as we've always done!"

* * *

Muireall looked at James with raised brows. "You do not look enthusiastic."

"I'm not. Lucinda said her father is determined to introduce me to *good Philadelphia society*," he said with a scowl. "Lucinda laughs at me when I complain and tells me it's just a meal and some conversation."

Kirsty was beside Muireall in the carriage opposite James, who'd come to escort his sisters and Payden to Lucinda's father's home for a fancy and well-attended ball. Payden was yanking at his tie and moving his head from side to side.

"This is too tight, Muireall. I can't breathe," he said.

"Please quit your fidgeting and complaining. You're the Earl of Taviston. The persons you meet this evening may serve to be useful as you regain your properties and your place in society."

"Oh, Muireall. Don't be stuffing the boy's head full of nonsense. We have been here in Philadelphia some fifteen years. We are Americans," James said. "At some point, we may have to let some of it go."

"Not on my watch, damn you, James," Muireall said. "He is father's son and therefore the rightful heir to all the properties and the title of Taviston."

Kirsty looked out the window. "We're here."

James jumped out of the carriage and reached back to help her and Muireall. Kirsty looked up at the lights blazing from the windows as they made their way inside and spotted Lucinda looking magnificent in a rich red, sleek, low-cut gown. All eyes would be on her beside James in his dark suit with a vest made from the Taviston plaid with its burgundy threads. James walked across the foyer to his wife, where she stood smiling at him. He laid his hand on her waist, pulled her close, and kissed her cheek, staying in that position for a few moments and finally eliciting laughter from her.

"Is it necessary for you to accost your wife publicly? Perhaps just a kiss on her gloved hand would be most appropriate for a lady of her position," Henri Vermeal said.

James smirked at his father-in-law, continuing their long-standing animosity. "Ladies married to boxers don't mind a little public affection."

Kirsty walked up to Mr. Vermeal and stood on tiptoe to give him a kiss on the cheek. "Well, since you are the handsomest man in the room, I believe you are the one who deserves a kiss."

Lucinda's father really was very stuffy and usually grumpy, but Kirsty believed he loved his daughter desperately and was therefore learning to tolerate her husband's large and loud family. She thought he was a bit lonely since Lucinda had married and his sister, who'd kept house for him since his wife's death decades ago, had married her girlhood sweetheart.

Vermeal shook his head, his typical frown not quite in place. "Miss Thompson, you are looking radiant. Your dress suits you well."

Vermeal greeted Muireall and Payden, and the three of them wandered the vast public rooms soon to be filled with guests. Servants were opening wine bottles and checking a table in the center of the room filled with iced oysters, lobster claws, fresh strawberries, and cut and peeled oranges. She accepted a glass of champagne from a passing servant and drank it quickly before Muireall could make a comment. The room began to fill with guests all in their finery, as an invitation to become better acquainted with Henri Vermeal, whose Vermeal Industries included holdings in France, Spain, and England as well as extensive properties in Virginia, was a prize. And their James was somehow to become part of that fold.

Alexander's sister, Annabelle, stood with her parents across the filling ballroom and waved when she spotted Kirsty. They navigated their way through other guests until finally reaching each other with outstretched arms.

"It has been ages!" Annabelle said with a laugh, squeezing

Kirsty's hands and looking her up and down from head to toe. "Your dress is so beautiful!"

"I do love it. I bought it last year, but it didn't seem right for James's wedding and it's just been sadly hanging in the back of my cupboard until Lucinda said her father was hosting a ball. Your dress is beautiful too! We are the two prettiest girls at the party!"

Annabelle laughed. "Oh, how I've missed you. Tell me. Tell me everything that has happened before the dancing begins and I've got to dance with a friend of my cousins'. You remember Uncle Nathan and Aunt Isadora's son, Benjamin, don't you? Well, he's brought a friend home from college, and I'm to dance the first one with him. Aunt Isadora said he is very handsome and charming, but I've yet to meet him."

Kirsty pulled a laughing Annabelle to the side of the room where some chairs had been set up. They huddled together, pointing to mutual acquaintances and telling each other all the details the other had missed.

"You boarded the *Maybelle?*" Annabelle asked, her eyes wide. "And couldn't get off?"

"Just as you predicted." Kirsty shrugged and proceeded to tell the story from beginning to end. "And then he delivered our nephew, as I'm sure your parents told you. Our perfect and beautiful Jonathon," she said with a sigh. "He was very masterful and didn't stutter once."

"Mr. Watson? Alexander's friend Mr. Watson?" Annabelle said with a shake of her head. "I've met him several times, but he didn't impress me as someone masterful."

"Oh, but he is."

"Perhaps I should look for someone shy and masterful all at the same time," she sighed and then turned quickly. "You kissed him? And he was hardly dressed, and you were in his robe? Glory be. What was it like?"

"I can't stop thinking about it," she said and bent close to Annabelle. "He put his tongue in my mouth."

Annabelle's mouth dropped open in horror. "You are funning me."

"I'm not. One of his hands was on my bottom holding me to him, and the other one was holding the back of my head. I could feel his privates through my chemise against my stomach," she whispered.

"Oh," Annabelle said, her eyes wide. "Oh."

"It was . . . it made me want him in a way I hadn't considered. Like I'd been dying of thirst, and he was a cold lemonade in a frosty glass on a hot day. But more than that," she paused and glanced at her friend, "I don't think I would have stopped if he hadn't stopped us."

"You would have . . ."

"Yes. I think I would have. No matter that your mother and my sister and aunt have told us as we grew up that we must be chaste, I would have taken my clothes off, all of them, if he'd asked me to. It is a very powerful thing, Annabelle." She shook her head. "I don't wonder now when I've heard about a young woman being disgraced because she'd been with a man. It would have been easy to do."

"And men must feel that too. But Mr. Watson was a gentleman. He stopped the two of you from doing anything you may have regretted," she said. "I think he must care about you, Kirsty."

"When he asked me to marry him, he said he was 'enamored' with me."

Annabelle smiled. "I can easily see him falling in love with you. Your smile and the way you make others feel so comfortable, let alone that you are quite beautiful. Yes. I can see him, as shy and quiet as he is, being drawn to you."

"It's odd. A few weeks ago, I'd just met him, and now I can't stop thinking about him."

"How romantic," Annabelle said with a sigh and then stood

quickly. "Oh. Here comes Cousin Benjamin with his friend. He's very handsome, is he not?"

Kirsty laughed and kissed her friend's cheek. "He is. Enjoy," she said and slipped away to find Muireall and Payden.

"INDEED, IT IS A PLEASURE TO FIND OTHERS OF OUR SAME SOCIAL set here in America," Althea Watson said as Albert escorted her through the receiving line. Henri Vermeal bowed over her hand. "I was so pleased to receive your invitation. I am Lady Watson, and this is my son, Sir Albert Watson."

"A pleasure, madam," Vermeal said. "Allow me to introduce my daughter, Mrs. Lucinda Vermeal Thompson, and her husband, Mr. James Thompson."

"*Sir* Albert," Thompson said, amused, and shook his hand.

He wasn't a "sir." His father was the one made a baronet, and that minor title did not confer a title to a son. He was plain old Mr. Watson, but his mother had long ago declared that Americans would never know that and insisted the royal family would want him to continue in his father's "glorious honor." But he was loath to stop her or embarrass her.

Mrs. Thompson was speaking to his mother, or rather listening to his mother, as she made her English roots and connections known. He hated escorting her to any social function, but he'd easily capitulated when she'd mentioned their invitation was to Henri Vermeal's home, as he was hoping Kirsty would be there. He missed her. It was strange to think that he'd only known her for a few short weeks and their separation felt unnatural to him. As if he'd known her for years. As if he should be able to tell her all the mundane things from his day and hear how she'd spent her time.

He looked around the room and saw her just as she met her sister and younger brother. She turned to glance at whatever her sister was gesturing to and saw him. She smiled at him, a full, glowing smile, telling him she was as happy to see him as he was her. His heart stuttered in his chest.

"Now you must escort me to meet some of your friends," his mother said, wrapping her hand around his elbow and looking around the room. "That young woman there. She is smiling at you. Do you know her? Otherwise, it would be highly improper for her to be signaling an unmarried gentleman in such a way."

"Things are not so strict here in America as they were when you met father in London."

"Of course not. Americans know nothing of good behavior."

He took a deep breath and led his mother to the Thompsons. "Please allow me to introduce you to my mother, Mrs. Watson. Mother, this is Miss Muireall Thompson, Miss Kirsty Thompson, and Mr. Payden Thompson. Their sister Elspeth is married to my good friend Alexander Pendergast, whom you've met several times, and you've just met their brother Mr. James Thompson, Mr. Vermeal's son-in-law."

"How nice to meet you, Mrs. Watson," Kirsty said with a smile.

"Actually, it is Lady Watson. My husband was awarded a baronetcy by the queen for his service to her family."

"Oh. Then it is nice to meet you, Lady Watson," Kirsty said with a smile. "What services did he perform?"

"Sir Wendell was a much sought-after physician in London. He cared for many in the queen's circle and in the royal family. He was even present for several of the royal births."

"What brought you to America?" Muireall asked.

"My husband was asked, begged really, to come teach at the new Harvard Medical School near Boston." She took a black hankie from her bag and dabbed her eyes. "He was doing what he loved best when he was overcome by a weakened heart."

Kirsty glanced at him, questions in her eyes, but quickly turned back to his mother. "You must miss your husband desperately. How long has it been since he passed away?"

"He went to the arms of his Maker on April sixteenth," she said with a sniff.

"Oh dear, Lady Watson. Just a few months ago," Kirsty said. "I'm so very sorry."

"The spring of 1862 was a dreadful time for our family, was it not, Albert?"

"It was, but it has been eight years now, and we've carried on."

"As your sainted father would have wanted."

Albert could tell that Muireall was squeezing her brother's arm tightly. Undoubtedly, a boy of his age, probably sixteen or so, found his mother ridiculous. *He* often found his mother ridiculous. But the young man was doing his best to keep his face appropriately solemn. The sisters glanced at each other as his mother bent her head and touched her nose with her handkerchief. He closed his eyes briefly, feeling certain that a young woman like Kirsty would be put off by his mother's histrionics, but when he opened his eyes, Kirsty was smiling at him, just as she always did.

"Mr. Watson? Would you be so kind as to escort my brother to the buffet tables? I thought perhaps your mother would like to be seated for a time with us and our Aunt Murdoch. Ma'am? Would you like to sit a moment? The receiving line was terribly long," Muireall said.

His mother smiled. Actually smiled. It was shocking since he couldn't remember the last time he'd seen her smile.

"I would like to sit for a moment, but I don't wish to monopolize you young girls' time. I'm sure there are several young men you'd rather be speaking to," she said.

"Nonsense." Kirsty slid her arm through his mother's. "There is only one gentleman I'm interested in talking to, but he is busy doing an errand for a friend." She leaned close to his mother and said in a mock whisper, "Men. They are never available when we need them!"

Albert was watching the three women as they walked away to

a grouping of chairs when Kirsty turned her head over her shoulder and winked at him. *He* was the only gentlemen she was interested in talking to she told him with that wink, and that made all his embarrassment over his mother fade away. He could see where the old aunt was sitting and his mother leaning rather heavily on Kirsty. She was just fifty years old and in good health as far as he could tell, but she looked twenty years older in her black gowns and hats, walking slowly, as if she were an invalid.

Payden, the young earl, was looking at him. "Women are a conundrum."

"Yes. You are exactly right; however, I don't see any way of living our lives without them," he said.

"I'm hungry." Thompson walked directly to where a servant was filling small plates. "I'll take two, please," the young man said.

"And how did you find yourself in Philadelphia, Lady Watson?" Muireall asked after the introduction to Aunt Murdoch. Kirsty glared at her aunt, who often was less than complimentary about Londoners.

"After Sir Wendell died, I decided to move here, where Albert had been accepted to study at the Philadelphia College of Medicine. Of course, I would have preferred to move back to London, but Albert was adamant that he would stay here regardless, and I could not leave my child here to fend for himself."

Murdoch rolled her eyes, and Kirsty hurried to speak. "It is quite noble of you to put aside your own wishes for your son," she said and earned a quick nod from Althea Watson. "But Philadelphia is a lovely city, and I imagine, as Lady Watson, you've found company you're accustomed to."

"I don't venture out much. Albert purchased a very satisfactory home for us, which I'm quite pleased with. I attend Sunday services, and thankfully there's an Episcopal church with many former Londoners in attendance close by."

Murdoch harrumphed. "The Church of England," she said with a thick brogue. "Not Christ-like in my opinion."

"I thought I heard the north when you spoke," Lady Watson said with a brittle smile. "So often the Scots were too inebriated to make their land work profitably, and many landed here, hoping for a less . . . rigorous lifestyle, from what I understand."

"The Clearances took many a good family from earning a living to adopting out their children as they'd not enough to feed them." Murdoch leaned forward. "Fortunes be, my family didn't have to worry about that as we own plenty of good farmland with hearty neighbors able to farm parcels of it at a healthy profit and still make their rent."

Kirsty glanced at Muireall, who'd laid a hand on Murdoch's arm. It was not widely known that Payden was the Earl of Taviston and rightful owner of Dunacres, a wealthy and prosperous property encompassing ten thousand acres, some of which was crop farmed and some supporting sheep and cattle. Their father had opposed the Clearances but did help those that wanted to emmigrate to America and had lost their livelihood from other properties.

"Owned farmland? Whatever brought you here, if you're landowners? Even Scottish ones," Lady Watson said dismissively.

Aunt Murdoch growled as Muireall responded.

"Our father and mother brought us here to see the country, and both passed away on the journey over. We landed in New York and eventually settled in Philadelphia. Payden was just a babe in arms," she said smoothly, repeating their oft told tale.

"But why . . . ?" Lady Watson began.

"And here comes Mr. Watson and Payden. And carrying a plate each for Aunt Murdoch and Lady Watson," Kirsty said and glanced up at Mr. Watson. "Tell us how you met Alexander."

But before he could answer, James joined their group and held out his hand to Muireall. "Lucinda is opening the dancing with her father, and I'm to join them on the dance floor with a partner.

And don't give me that twaddle that you are too old to dance. Come along, Sister."

"Miss Thompson?" Mr. Watson said. "Would you care to dance?"

"You are done with your errand for a friend?" she asked him with a teasing smile.

He nodded and glanced at his mother, who was staring at her. "I am," he said.

Once on the dance floor, she reached up to place one hand on his shoulder and her other in his, and he led her into a slow turn. She smiled up at him, suddenly so glad to be with him, to be private with him, even if it was on a crowded dance floor. "I think you should call me Kirsty." She glanced at the other dancers whirling past them. "We are going rather slow, are we not?"

"We are." He cleared his throat. "Any faster and there is danger my feet will be tangled and we'll p-pitch head long into the buffet table."

She laughed and tilted her head, seeing the blush on his face. "Then this is exactly the speed I would like to go."

"How was Mother?"

"She likes to make sure everyone is aware of her consequence. And she and Aunt Murdoch may come to blows while we are all dancing."

"I h-hope she was not insulting. She can be, I'm sorry to say."

Kirsty shrugged. "There are always unpleasant people in the world and that we often must deal with, sometimes regularly. Sometimes they are lonely or hurt. We don't always know how a person feels or why they feel that way." She glanced at him from under her lashes. "But we can't allow their behavior to influence ours, can we?"

"I don't know," he said cautiously. "I've recently realized I've found her behavior easier to avoid than d-deal with."

"She's staring at us rather intently as we dance." She giggled. "Have you noticed?"

He barked a laugh. "Mostly because you led her to believe I was the gentleman you were interested in talking to."

"But you are," she said soberly. "I have been thinking all day of having a chance to speak with you tonight."

"I-I feel the s-same. And I've yet to tell you how v-very beautiful you look."

"Thank you."

As if by mutual design, they walked through the open paned-window doors, out onto the patio, and into the garden. They walked into the deep shadows of the trees, where she stopped and turned to him.

"Will you kiss me, Albert?" she whispered.

He bent his head and touched his lips to hers. It was as if fireworks went off inside of her, leaving her breathless and wanting much more of him. She put her hands on his shoulders and stood on her tiptoes to be closer as his hands tightened at her waist. He moaned as their tongues touched and she drew his into her mouth.

"There you are, Kirsty," they heard and jumped apart. Lucinda was walking toward them slowly. "Oh, Mr. Watson! I didn't see you there; it is so dark in this part of the garden. You'll have to excuse us, but my father is asking for Kirsty. I think he wants to introduce you to someone who does some importing for him. He thought you might be able to talk to them about your ideas for Scottish wool and yarn."

"Oh! How wonderful," she said and looked up at Mr. Watson. "Will you excuse me, sir?"

He nodded, and she was soon bundled away by her sister-in-law.

# CHAPTER 9

"Here she is," Vermeal said, taking Kirsty's hand in his. "She's sister-in-law to Lucinda and a lovely, bright girl. Miss Kirsty Thompson, this is Mr. Donald Cartwright and his business partner, Mr. Pierre Arnaud." The shorter of the two men, dressed in a pale blue coat, glanced at Mr. Vermeal. "We're dispensing with the honorifics. You are just plain old Mr. Arnaud here in Philadelphia."

Mr. Arnaud bowed over her hand. "Mademoiselle Thompson. How fortunate I am to meet the most beautiful woman at the ball."

"You are exaggerating, Mr. Arnaud, but you may repeat it as often as you'd like," she said with a laugh. "I am honored to meet you both."

"Henri tells us you are interested in importing Scottish wools and yarn. What are your plans?"

"I've met with several seamstresses and clothing makers who believe they could sell dresses and coats made from Highland wool and set their knitters to making shawls and scarves from the yarn. There's plenty of Scots here in Philadelphia and, of course, those who wish they were."

Donald Cartwright laughed. "Well said, Miss Thompson. My grandparents came from Argyll here with my father and his sisters during the Revolution and have never regretted it. Other than having to kill other Highlanders conscripted to the British when they landed in Boston."

"Think how charmed these store owners and seamstresses would be when they meet Mademoiselle Thompson. She will sell more than we can ship to her with just one little smile," Arnaud said with a faint French accent. "Don't you agree, Donald?"

"I do," he said and stepped closer to her. "Why don't we meet on Monday, and we'll have a fine luncheon and discuss the kind of contract that would benefit you the most."

"What time shall we meet, gentlemen?" Vermeal asked and raised his brows as the two men looked at him. "Well, certainly you didn't think Miss Thompson would be friendless? That she wouldn't have someone experienced in contractual matters to give her suggestions and warn her of potential pitfalls?"

Kirsty hid her surprise and smiled up at Mr. Vermeal. He was playing the gallant, but she was well aware that she would not understand the legal terms of the contract. She'd planned on finding a lawyer willing to read it and advise her before she signed anything or maybe speak to Alexander about it. But this was better. Lucinda's father would be a savvy negotiator, and he already had experience dealing with these two men.

Cartwright stepped back and glanced at Vermeal. "Of course, Henri. I expected nothing less. We'll send round a note with the time to meet, Miss Thompson."

"Thank you, gentlemen. I'm looking forward to hearing your thoughts on how you could be of service to me." She smiled and reached out her hand. Cartwright shook it, and Arnaud kissed it and winked at her. Both men turned and walked away.

Vermeal let out a low chuckle. "Brilliant, my dear. Always keep the ones you're negotiating with aware of who holds the cards." He turned to her then, looking serious. "I know how you modern young ladies want to be independent. I did not mean to presume, and if you would prefer to meet them alone or with just a chaperone, I'll send a note saying I've another meeting I could not miss."

"Absolutely not. I did not want to bother you with something so mundane as my little idea, but if you're inclined, I would like you to come with me. I've no understanding of contracts and know I would need help."

"What are you smiling about, Father?" Lucinda asked as she walked up to them, James at her side.

"Who were those two men, Kirsty?" James asked.

"They are importers Mr. Vermeal has introduced to me. They may be able to help me import the products I want. I'm to meet with them Monday, and your father-in-law has offered to come along and review the contract they may present."

"Will you need a chaperone?"

"I'm going to ask Muireall. One look from her can set anyone back on their heels," Kirsty said.

"She can be a disconcerting female to someone who does not know her," James agreed.

"My thoughts also," Kirsty said.

Lucinda nodded across the room. "I believe Mr. Watson is leaving."

"Oh, oh, I would like to speak to him before he goes." Kirsty pardoned herself. But before she was far, Mr. Cartwright approached her.

"The orchestra is tuning up to begin again. Will you partner me? I believe it is a waltz."

Kirsty looked up at him. It would certainly be good to get to know him a bit more before their meeting because, for as gentlemanly as he appeared, she believed he would be a devil to negotiate with. She glanced over her shoulder and saw Albert looking at her over the heads of other guests until his mother tapped his arm and they both turned to the door. *Drat!*

Kirsty hurried to the doorway after finishing the dance with

Mr. Cartwright. There was something she didn't care for about the man, but she could not worry about it now. She wanted to tell Albert about her upcoming meeting. She was excited and petrified at the same time, thinking she was one step closer to opening her warehouse, and there was no one she wanted to share all those feelings with more than Albert Watson. His mother was standing near the door speaking to another older woman, a servant helping her with her wrap.

"Lady Watson?" she said as she approached. The woman turned to her, losing whatever smile she had on her face when speaking to the older woman. "I wanted to say good night to you and to Mr. Watson. I hope you enjoyed yourself."

"Mr. Vermeal's hospitality is unimpeachable, of course. It is quite unfortunate for that gentleman to have his daughter tie herself to an uncouth ruffian, a burden to his family and fortune."

"That is my brother you are speaking of, ma'am," she said, working to keep her temper in check.

Lady Watson looked her over, from her hair to her shoes. "Of course, I'm aware of that. It is what I told my son. Be careful he does not attach himself to a young woman intent on separating him from his nearest and dearest. And of course, he would not want to make the mistake of falling for a pretty face hoping to raise herself in society."

Ah, how words could pierce a victory. She noticed Albert then, speaking to an older man and a young woman. Feeling deflated, she did not want to talk to him just then. He would wonder why, and she would undoubtedly blurt out his mother's comment and, by doing so, fulfill that woman's prophecy. She turned hurriedly, with only a nod to his mother, and made her way quickly through the throng to Muireall's side.

ALBERT SPENT A RESTLESS NIGHT IN HIS LIBRARY, A BRANDY beside him, intent on reading a new medical journal and failing miserably. Whoever the fellow was who led Kirsty out on the dance floor as he and his mother were claiming their wraps in the foyer of the Vermeal mansion was a handsome, suave, well-built devil. He didn't like it. Not one bit. But what was he to do about it? He was an academic, and his brief time guarding Kirsty Thompson had taught him how ill-equipped he was. What would he have been able to do if those men on the ship or at the train station had managed to get their hands on her? Would he have been able to defend her? He didn't believe he could have. He was strong enough, he thought, but not fast enough and certainly lacking in skills.

The next morning, he dressed, ate, and sent Clawson to the library to fetch books he needed and told him to take the rest of the day for himself. The young man made himself available every day and every hour; Albert thought he meant to make himself as useful as possible as if to repay Albert with his time and devotion. He would have to be as kind to himself as he intended to be to Clawson in the future. But in the meantime, he intended to beard the lion in his den.

The Thompson Sporting Arena was massive and had a hive of workmen pounding and painting and building. Alexander had told him the story of Thompson's retirement from the ring, how he'd been beaten badly in a match and taken months to recover, eventually winning his rematch. Lucinda had objected strenuously to his profession and he quit the ring, accepted investors like Alexander and his father, and was now in the process of building a sportsman's arena and training academy.

He found James Thompson in the center of all of the activity, several men surrounding him as he showed them something on a large piece of paper, presumably a drawing. Albert waited as James spoke to the men and looked at the massive sets of seating being built and at the large doors he'd just come through, well able to handle a large surge of customers. The ceiling must have been thirty feet off the floor, and large paned windows covered the top ten or so feet of the walls, allowing the room to be flooded with daylight. Gas lamps hung suspended from the ceiling, for darker days or evenings, he imagined.

James turned to point at something and noticed him standing there. Albert turned his hat in his hand, suddenly unsure of himself. The men surrounding Thompson dispersed, and he walked toward Albert in that loose-limbed, cocky way he had—and that Albert admitted to himself he envied.

"Watson. What brings you here?"

"I've a favor to ask."

Thompson's brows rose. "A favor? From me?"

"I would like to learn to box."

"Box? What on earth for?"

"I . . . I want to know what to do if need to defend myself. Or another person."

James studied him. "Like my sister?"

"Yes. Like your sister."

"Still thinking you might marry her?"

"I have never withdrawn my proposal, nor would I."

"If you're thinking about defending her against the people that are after our family, then you need to learn to fight, not box."

"There's a difference?"

"There's rules in boxing. When you're fighting for your life or for hers, there are no rules. There is no gentlemanly behavior, there is only what will kill your opponent before you are killed."

"I don't necessarily want to kill someone. I just want to look intimidating," he whispered. "Could we speak about this in private?"

James laughed. "Here's your first lesson. Don't ask a question. State your business and what you want. Instead of asking me to speak in private, just say 'we'll speak about this privately.'"

Albert straightened his shoulders. "We'll speak about this in private."

"Look me in the eye when you say it."

He cleared his throat and looked up. "We'll speak in private."

"Better," James said. "Follow me."

ALBERT DRAGGED HIMSELF HOME AND UP TO HIS ROOMS LATER that day, still sweating and sore in some places he had not known could cause pain. He filled the tub in his bathing room and sank into the blissfully hot water. He'd just finished soaping his hair when there was a knock at the door.

"Mr. Watson? Are you all right, sir? Lady Watson said you've been home for over an hour, and Mr. Graybell said you've been in your bathing room ever since."

"I'm fine, Mr. Clawson. You may come in if you want," he said. He'd been humiliated all day, what would it matter if his secretary saw him naked?

The door cracked open, and Clawson peeked in. "Dear Lord, sir. What has happened to your face?"

"An excellent question. I am learning to box. No. I must correct that. I'm learning to fight."

"Does your face hurt?"

"Yes. Would you see if Mrs. Munchin has any ice in the house? I would like to reduce the swelling before my injuries are unsightly."

"Your pardon, sir, but that particular ship has left the dock."

Albert harrumphed a laugh and then winced as his lip began to bleed again. "And some of that ointment she uses for household cuts."

Only a few minutes later, Albert heard the door to his sleeping room open and close and some loud whispering.

"Perhaps the master needs a doctor, Mr. Clawson."

"He *is* a doctor, sir. If he needed assistance, he would ask, as he has done by asking for ice."

"I can hear you," Albert said. "Bring the ice, please. I can no longer feel my cheek."

Both men came through the door, Graybell gasping when he saw him. Albert stood, letting the water run off him, realizing he felt less self-conscious of his nakedness than normal, accepting the towel Graybell handed to him and wrapping it around his waist. These were other men, just as there had been at the large training area that was already complete and open for athletes of all kinds to work on their sport. The dressing room had been filled with men in various stages of undress, some even naked. It had been a bit unnerving at first when Thompson had handed him a loose-fitting shirt and tight pants with a drawstring waist and told him to change. Thompson had noted how short the pants were on Albert and how tall he was with enough blasphemies to turn the heads of the other men in the room.

"I went to the Thompson Sporting Arena today to ask Mr. Thompson for some instructions on how to defend myself, if necessary," he said with a look at Clawson and a quick shake of his head.

"You didn't speak to Mr. James Thompson, did you, sir? Of course not. I'm sure the champion is too busy . . ."

"I did speak to him, and he has agreed to help me train."

"James Thompson? The bareknuckle champion?" Graybell asked, a hand at his throat.

"He is brother to the young lady I'm courting," Albert said, following James's suggestion that he must speak as if what he wished to be were real, or nearly so.

"One of the Thompson sisters?" Graybell said, eyes wide. "The middle daughter has married into the Pendergast family, I understand. Is this the eldest sister, sir?"

Albert dried his hair and pulled on his short drawers. He sat and accepted Graybell's ministrations with Mrs. Munchin's dreadful-smelling ointment. "No. The youngest sister."

Graybell's eyebrows rose. "Ah. The beauty of the family. Well done, sir."

"It seems you know quite a bit about the Thompsons."

"Everyone in Philadelphia, especially those in service, are familiar with the Thompsons. He's a champion boxer, and the whole family is quite well respected. Carry themselves as if they are lords and ladies from the old country, sir, with none of the snobbery. The eldest has single-handedly saved the orphanage at the Sisters of Charity, and she's not even Catholic!"

"What did you learn today, sir?" Clawson asked.

"Thompson had me doing exercises and stretching and lifting weights. And then we sparred. That is how my face came to look as it does. The man's hands move so fast I barely see his fists coming. I'm going to follow the regimen he has shown me here and visit the arena for further instruction."

Clawson opened his mouth to speak and quickly turned away.

"What is it?" Albert asked.

"If it would not be a bother, I would like to watch what you do so that I might improve myself," Clawson said. "I've never recovered my strength after my accident, and I imagine it will only become more difficult as I age."

Albert smiled. "Of course you may. As a matter of fact, I was thinking of ordering a set of weights for here. Perhaps there is a room, Graybell, that could be commandeered for a private training room for Mr. Clawson and me?"

"Absolutely," Mr. Graybell replied. "A student of James Thompson in our household! What a blessing. What an honor!"

"I'll want to have a large variety of wools on hand, so I'll need a small warehouse or showroom to store them," Kirsty said as she sipped her soup in the fine dining rooms of the Chestnut Hill Hotel. Mr. Vermeal had picked her up in his fancy carriage, and she had dressed with care that morning, choosing a fine outfit suitable for the daytime, no frills or bows, and businesslike in its style. She did not want Mr. Arnaud or Mr. Cartwright thinking her a featherheaded miss.

"That is a good strategy, Miss Thompson," Cartwright said. "But inventory can be expensive to maintain and store. Perhaps we could unburden you of those risks and carry the inventory in our warehouses."

Vermeal shook his head. "Miss Thompson's capital investment will be quite sufficient without paying a broker. I think she will be most satisfied if you see to the shipping and delivery of the product she's ordered."

Thankfully, Mr. Vermeal had asked a few pertinent questions on the way to the dining rooms and understood what she needed from the men. "That's correct, sir. I've already established a relationship with the manufacturers. I need someone to pick up the goods and deliver them to me."

"But we were so hoping that we could make some small investment in your venture," Arnaud said with a smile, leaning close to her as he did. Vermeal looked pointedly at Arnaud's hand where it had covered hers.

"What a lovely offer, gentlemen. I'm flattered. But at this time, I'm relying on my family to invest, which they have already agreed to."

Mr. Cartwright continued to smile, but his eyes were cold as he looked at her. "How fortunate you are to have a family financially able to invest without stretching a household budget thin."

"We won't be discussing the Thompson finances, Mr. Cartwright," Muireall said with a thin-lipped half smile. "That soup was delicious."

"It certainly was, Miss Thompson," Vermeal said and popped a bite of roll into his mouth.

Discussion of the contract began then in more specific terms, and Mr. Vermeal shook his head a few times, indicating a change must be made. She'd told him in the carriage on the way to their appointment to feel free to interject any comments or questions on her behalf, and perhaps the negotiations would be quicker than she'd anticipated. He was very skilled in his conversations with the two men, conceding on what she imagined he thought were unimportant points and standing firm on others. She paid close attention to his methods of persuasion, knowing that she'd need those skills in all other aspects of her business.

Her business! She could hardly contain herself! She'd almost convinced herself that her dreams were unattainable and that she would forever be the useless child in an extraordinary family. How would she ever compete with Muireall as the head of the family, James as the protector, Elspeth as its heart, and Payden as the heir to the family throne? Her occasional histrionics and tears and muddle-headedness would fade from memory as she succeeded, and she *would* succeed and prove that she was as worthy of the Thompson name as the others.

# CHAPTER 10

"Get up, Watson," James Thompson said.

Albert raised himself on his elbows and shook his head, sweat flying from his face and hair. He was wondering why he was putting himself through the pain and agony he'd endured for the last few weeks when he sparred with Kirsty Thompson's brother. There was a reason the man was considered the champ, even though he'd officially retired. The other men at the gymnasium looked at Albert jealously as he had personal training time with Thompson, no doubt wondering what there could possibly be about him that would prompt the boxer to spend any amount of time on training a man, especially one who was tall, thin, slow, and not terribly coordinated.

He pushed himself to his feet and brought his hands up as Thompson had taught him, bent his knees slightly, and moved one foot forward for balance.

"Jesus, Mary, and all the Saints!" James dropped his hands to his sides. "By the time you got yourself organized, I could have slit your throat."

Albert blew out a breath. "I don't think I'll ever be any good at this."

"No. You definitely won't. But I can see that the weights and other exercises have made a difference. You've added quite a bit of muscle to your arms and chest, although you had plenty of muscle to start with; it's only that your damn limbs are so long I could hardly tell."

"Mr. Watson! Whatever are you doing here?"

Albert turned quickly, seeing Kirsty Thompson hurrying across the training room floor, Elspeth Pendergast trailing behind. He lunged for his shirt and pulled it over his head, his face reddening.

"What are you doing here, Kirsty?" Thompson asked with a laugh. He turned to Elspeth. "Shouldn't you be home with my nephew rather than aiding our sister in her shenanigans?"

"I am happily a mother, but I am also a sister, James. Jonathon can manage with only his nurse and his father for a few hours."

"Mr. Watson?" Kirsty repeated.

Albert bent down to let himself out of the ropes surrounding the ring and nearly tripped, just catching himself on one hand. He straightened and walked to her, tucking his shirt into his pants as best he could. There was nothing to be done about his bare feet. "Miss Thompson. Mrs. Pendergast."

"Mr. Watson," Elspeth replied with a smile. "You have a bit of blood on your chin, I think."

Albert turned away, using his sleeve to wipe his lip.

"James!" Kirsty shouted. "How could you? You've hurt him, and he's not a fighter like you. He could never keep up with you, and you know it! How cruel!"

"Your words could cut a man to the bone, Kirsty! Good God! He does fine with his weight training! Just not so fast with his fists."

"Lower your voices, please," Elspeth said and glanced around at the faces turned their way. She looked up at Albert. "I do admire a person willing to try something new. I do assume training with my brother is new as opposed to lecturing at a university and delivering a friend's baby."

"It is new, Mrs. Pendergast. How is little Jonathon doing?" he said, feeling sweat roll down his neck and onto his chest.

"Oh, he is well. Lively, sleeps well, and has an affinity for his father that I'm coming to resent." She laughed. She glanced at Kirsty, who was still staring at him, and turned to her brother. "Kirsty wants you to come with her to view a storefront for her fabrics, and as we'd just had our luncheon with your wife, she told us you were here, and we decided to stop by so she could ask you personally. Kirsty?"

"Lucinda was out and about with you?" James asked.

"She was." Elspeth said and stared at him knowingly. "She even had some soup and tea."

Thompson glanced away and blew out a breath. "Should I . . . do you think I should go home to her? Is she feeling well?"

It was encouraging to see a man as confident as James Thompson be unsettled, unsure of himself. Albert would guess his wife was expecting a child and he was at sixes and sevens as to how to act. And even to his inexperienced eyes in matters of the heart, it was obvious that Thompson loved his wife desperately, worshipped her, was maybe even a bit in awe of her.

"She's fine," Elspeth said. "She is in good hands and was going to lay down for a rest when we left."

"Wednesday, James. First thing. On Fourth Street. Will you come?" Kirsty asked.

"Of course I'll come," he said. "Now out with you both. Watson and I need to finish his training."

"Do you think Mr. Watson was injured and too proud to tell us?" Kirsty asked as soon as Elspeth's driver had closed the carriage door.

"No, dear. You are worrying too much. James would not intentionally hurt him more than the man could manage—unless he was in the ring for a match."

"I just don't understand why he would be doing it," Kirsty said. "Boxing, I mean. Lifting up weights, as James mentioned. Why? He is a scholar and has no need to be a brute."

"Kirsty, dear. He is doing it for you, I imagine. I think he was very upset about those men who followed you on the *Maybelle*. I think he felt inadequate. It does not help, of course, that you continue to talk about him as if he is not manly."

"He is manly," Kirsty said and pulled at the strings on her bag. "It's just that he's not anything like James or Alexander, or even MacAvoy."

"Of course he isn't. He is cerebral in nature rather than physical. That does not mean he is any less of a man. He's just different," she said and leaned close. "Do you find him attractive?"

Kirsty groaned. She could not help it. "Oh yes, Elspeth. I think about how he kissed me in New York all the time, and then today he had no shirt on. I find him very attractive."

"Then perhaps be a bit more gentle with him. He does not seem the type to be overly sensitive, but still, men do not like to hear their faults said publicly. I venture women don't either, but sadly some become accustomed to it."

"He's probably used to it too. Wait until you meet his mother," Kirsty said and Elspeth laughed.

"Muireall said she was 'mildly unpleasant' but suspected she was holding back her natural tendencies."

"That was the kindest thing she could say," Kirsty said. "She is the type of woman always looking for a way to show her superiority. Not that she bothered me."

Kirsty was silent then, even as the usually quiet Elspeth chattered about her son and her husband, knowing that her interactions with Lady Watson were weighing heavily on her mind. She nodded or smiled when appropriate, but finally when they turned onto Locust Street, she blurted out another question.

"How did you know that you loved Alexander?"

Elspeth smiled shyly. "I don't think there was just a moment when I realized it, it was more a slow change in how I viewed others and the world itself. He was never far from my thoughts, what he was doing or where he was. Whether I would dance with him, or even," she said softly and swallowed, "if I would ever see him again. I thought of all of you and how much I loved each of you while I was kidnapped by Plowman's men and in that dreadful room. But I saw his face in my mind's eye and heard his voice as if he were beside me, especially as I gripped that dagger in my skirts."

"I did not mean to dredge up dreadful memories. I am sorry."

"Don't be. It is worse, I think, when others never mention it. As if it never happened. It happened. I knew I loved Alexander prior to that night, but perhaps I did not realize how deeply until then, even though I needed considerable time afterward to be comfortable with him, or really with anyone other than our family."

The carriage rolled to a halt, and the driver jumped down from his seat to open the door. Kirsty hesitated.

"I can't stop thinking about him. About the last time I saw him and what he said and what I said." She looked up at Elspeth. "I wish I could see him, talk to him, every day. I also cannot stop thinking of his mother, Lady Watson. She is a miserable person and was so intent on making Aunt Murdoch uncomfortable when we were at the Vermeals'."

"You must allow his courtship, if for no other reason than to see if your feelings are real or fleeting. I didn't meet his mother, though Muireall told me some of the conversation." She glanced at her with raised brows. "Give Aunt Murdoch a kiss for me. I've got to be home shortly to feed Jonathon. I love you, dearest."

Kirsty waved as the door to the carriage closed. "I love you too."

. . .

*Dear Miss Thompson,*

*I'm hoping you'd like to take a walk in State House Square one afternoon this week. I'm interested in hearing about your meeting that Mr. Vermeal arranged, if you are inclined to tell me. Would this Saturday at two in the afternoon suit?*

*Sincerely,*
*Albert Watson*

KIRSTY HAD PENNED A QUICK NOTE AND SENT IT BACK WITH the messenger. Of course she would like to see him, she thought and hugged her arms about herself. It seemed the day would never arrive, but it finally did. She wore a new dress, cream with delicate embroidered violets on the sheer overdress and a lilac-colored velvet belt. Her straw hat was tilted to one side of her head with the same velvet trim as her dress, and a few silk violets adorned the brim. She was in good looks, she thought as she checked her appearance in the mirror. She heard the front door open and hurried down the steps.

"Miss Thompson," Mr. Watson said and handed her a bouquet of flowers. "These are f-for you."

"Why, thank you." She beamed at him and turned to Mrs. McClintok. "Would you put these in water for me, please?"

The housekeeper nodded at her after glancing at Mr. Watson. "Certainly, Miss Thompson. Mr. Graham has sent word that at least one of his men will be following you."

"Thank you, Mrs. McClintok." She turned to Mr. Watson. "Shall we go? It's a beautiful day."

"Allow me to help you in, Miss Thompson," he said when they reached his carriage.

"We had decided, had we not, to use our Christian names, and then we did not see each other for several weeks and we are back to Miss and Mister. You're welcome to call me Kirsty again."

"Thank you. Please call me Albert. I have never had the

opportunity to thank you for being so kind to my mother," he said after seating himself and picking up the reins of the carriage. "She can be . . . difficult."

"That was clear, although I don't mean to offer disrespect," she said. "She is very proud of her place in society, both here and in England. How will she feel when you marry, when there is another woman who is part of your life?"

"She is . . . well, I've recently realized that she may be an impediment to any courtship I may have, although she tells me that she realizes I will eventually marry."

"Courtship you *may* have?" Kirsty glanced at him. "Are you saying you are planning a courtship with someone else?"

"Good Lord, no! This is quite enough."

"Thank you for your bluntness, sir." Kirsty turned her head to watch the passing scenery. Her throat was suddenly tight, and she blinked away the coming tears. She was not really *for* anyone, was she, she asked herself and then noticed the carriage had pulled off to the side of the street.

"Miss Thompson. Kirsty. That is not what I meant at all." He took her hands in his, starting down at them as he rubbed his thumb over the back of her lace glove.

"Albert?"

"I didn't mean that you were 'quite enough,'" he said finally. "It's just that I am so bad at this, and you are so b-beautiful and clever and so far above my reach; I get nervous and don't know quite what to do or say and end up saying the wrong thing. I think about you all the time and have neglected my work d-dreadfully. I am smitten, Kirsty." He glanced up at her. "Tell me what I must do to make it up to you."

"Oh, Albert," she whispered and tilted her head so the brim of her hat was out of the way and she was nose to nose with him. "You have just said everything that is necessary to be said. I have missed kissing you."

He stared at her mouth, his breath coming in short pants,

moving closer until his lips touched hers. She closed her eyes, giving herself up to the feelings, the intimacy of having his mouth on hers. His arm snaked around her waist, pulling her tight to him, hip to hip. He smelled of mint and soap and something that was uniquely Albert. His tongue touched her lips, and she moaned into his mouth, moving closer to him and cupping his cheek with her hand. Her lips closed around his tongue as she drew it inside her mouth. Albert made a guttural sound in his throat.

Her eyes flashed opened when she heard someone close by clear their throat. Albert blinked but did not move.

"Sorry to bother, Miss Thompson," Bamblebit said as she glanced at him. "You're starting to gather a crowd."

There was no mistaking the censure in his voice. He was one of Alexander's security men who'd been tasked this fine day with seeing to her safety. How mortifying!

"Oh dear. Mr. Watson, please continue on."

Albert blinked slowly, as if waking up from a dream. "What is it, Kirsty?"

"Mr. Bamblebit, the security man hired by Alexander, said we have gathered a crowd. Look around. But do it casually. People are staring! We were kissing right here in the street. At the entrance to busy, crowded park!"

Albert's eyes widened, and he cleared his throat. He picked up the reins and began to move the carriage forward just as some young men began to whistle and shout comments. She could feel her face redden.

"Wait until Muireall hears about this! She will bark at me as if I'm ten years old."

"I CANNOT APOLOGIZE ENOUGH FOR EXPOSING YOU TO GOSSIP, Miss Thompson."

"Are we back to Miss Thompson? Our mouths were sealed

together, just a few minutes ago on Front Street, with a crowd gathered to watch." She made an unhappy sound but continued to smile as passersby pointed and commented.

"We must marry immediately. I can't allow your good name to be sullied because I am unable to control my most base instincts," Albert said and shouted to a young man making inappropriate gestures. "Sod off!" He realized he'd lost control of the situation and of his temper, reverting back to the language of his youth.

"I will not be bullied into marriage, Albert. I will not. I'm on the cusp of beginning my own business, something I've dreamed about for years, and I'm not sure that I love you. I may, but I'm not positive, and I refuse to commit us to a union that might make us unhappy in the years to come."

His mouth was dry suddenly, and he could barely form words. "You . . . you m-might l-love me?"

He'd toyed with that word in his head, played with the idea that this woman would commit to a life with him, but he had refused to allow himself to consider love. He couldn't. He could not bear the disappointment. But here she was using that word. Even though she was unsure of herself and her feelings. He had no idea what to do.

"Please take me home," she said. "I must speak to my family before they hear this gossip from someone else."

He swung his carriage around and nodded at the man on horseback watching him. His looks made it clear that he would rather beat him to a bloody mess than follow them around as a duty to his employer. What a coil! He would just pray his mother did not hear. Kirsty jumped down from the carriage before he could help her and ran up the stone steps to the front of their Locust Street home. Bamblebit was still staring at him.

"That's no way to treat a lady, Watson," he said, turned his horse, and trotted away.

. . .

HOLLY BUSH

IT WAS A WEEK TO THE DAY AFTER THAT PUBLIC KISS THAT THE consequences really became clear. Muireall had been furious, of course, even as Aunt Murdoch had laughed. Alexander had interrogated her shortly after her arrival home that day on a most disturbing report from Bamblebit. He had been intent on paying Albert a visit until Elspeth convinced him it was up to Kirsty whether to interfere or not. No one was telling James anything.

But she was here now at the annual Ladies Luncheon sponsored by the Philadelphia Library Association. Elspeth had been solicited to become a board member with her elevation in society when she'd married Alexander. Muireall, Lucinda, and Kirsty had traveled together in Lucinda's carriage to meet Elspeth at the Philadelphia Hotel and stood in line with the other women, all clad in their finest day wear and hats. She refused to bow her head, and Lucinda, being accustomed to navigating social settings, linked arms with her and nodded regally to other women, occasionally stopping to talk and introduce her "dear sisters-in-law."

The meal was lovely and the speakers inspirational, talking about how the libraries' books had lifted them up or helped the downtrodden become more educated. Kirsty could see the end of the event coming, just the mingling left, where the board members spoke to prominent women about the size of their donations.

"Almost done," Lucinda said as she smiled and nodded at another cluster of women in the crowded room. "Stand tall. Smile."

It was just then that Lady Watson spotted her in the crowd, pointed a shaking finger across the room, and raised her voice. "You! Of all the cheek! To show your face with good Christian women!"

Kirsty froze. Even the ever-composed Lucinda faltered a moment. Elspeth wrapped her hand around her other arm, and the three women turned toward the door.

"That's her! That's the tramp who molested my son! Miss Kirsty Thompson! What do you have to say for yourself?"

Kirsty turned and took a step forward, dropping Elspeth's and Lucinda's hands from her arms. She stared at the woman, whose bosom was heaving with indignation as a crowd of women gathered around her, staring at Kirsty.

"I beg your pardon, Lady Watson? Molested your son?"

"It's not as though you were not seen pawing and grabbing at his person. Hussy!"

Kirsty turned to the door, her sister and sister-in-law flanking her, but stopped and turned back. She walked directly to his mother, who narrowed her eyes and grimaced as she approached.

"If you intended to bring shame on me or on my family, you may think you have succeeded, and perhaps you have, but more than that, you have shamed your own son, a fine man, a brilliant one," Kirsty said calmly. "We should have never embraced as we did publicly, but sometimes affianced couples are less proper than they should be when displaying their affection."

"Affianced!" the woman shrieked and pointed. "He would never align himself with a woman like yourself, lost to all good behavior. He is a gentleman!"

"And you are making a mockery of him by shouting like a madwoman," she said softly. She felt Muireall come up beside her.

"Lady Watson, won't you join us for tea one afternoon? Kirsty's entire family wishes to get to know Mr. Watson's family better, as they will soon be related, of course. My sister Elspeth Pendergast," Muireall said and paused to a low murmur of voices, "and my sister-in-law, Lucinda Vermeal Thompson, would also be in attendance. I'll send a note soon."

"An excellent idea, Muireall," Lucinda said and turned to Althea. "My father, Henri Vermeal, is an intimate to many in the royal family. Perhaps you and he have London friends in common and can speak of it more than when you met him in the receiving line at my family home. He'll be very glad to meet you again during the engagement festivities. Kirsty is like a second daughter to him."

Kirsty stared at Althea Watson. The crowd of women around her had thinned considerably, and some were looking at Althea askance. Kirsty turned to her family. "What a lovely lunch and such a good cause. It is so wonderful you are a board member, Elspeth. Good day, Lady Watson."

They seated themselves in Lucinda's spacious carriage, and Kirsty took a deep breath, calming her racing heart. What a scene!

"You can be such a snob when it is appropriate, Muireall." Elspeth laughed. "My sister Elspeth *Pendergast* and my sister in-law, Lucinda *Vermeal* Thompson.'"

"I do my best when faced with such a ridiculous person," Muireall said with a small smile. "And it wasn't as if it was hard to best her."

"Her face when you said you and Mr. Watson were affianced! I could barely keep from laughing at her!" Lucinda said.

"I was terribly embarrassed, and there was little I could say to defend myself. She was right about my behavior, but I hated to think people would think less of Albert. He doesn't deserve censure," she said. "And it was really very gratifying to watch her visibly shrink into that horrid black gown."

"I think you'd better marry the man soon," Lucinda said. "I think you're more than partial."

Muireall nodded. "And you were seen on the street kissing him."

Kirsty looked them each in the eye. "I'm not sure I could subject myself to a lifetime with his mother, though. If this is her typical behavior, it would be dreadful living with her, and I think it would drive a wedge of acrimony between Albert and me. I wonder now if I can do it."

"There is that," Elspeth said. "I'm so fortunate to have Alexander's parents, sister, and aunt and uncle as my in-laws.

They are wonderful and caring and accept me as one of their own. It would be extremely uncomfortable to be married to a man whose family you disliked, or if they disliked you. Dreadfully uncomfortable, especially living in the same house."

"But you can hardly allow her behavior to guide or influence your happiness," Muireall said. "Your plans to marry him are now publicly known, so you must come to some agreement with Mr. Watson about your living arrangements, and you absolutely must discuss your concerns with him. And you'd best face facts. You are going to marry Mr. Watson."

# CHAPTER 11

"It is a pity, is it not, about the gossip surrounding that young lady you seemed to be interested in. Thomas is her family name, I think," Frederick Masterson said to Albert as they were lunching together at the Philadelphia Club on Walnut Street.

Frederick was eating their famous veal-and-ham pie, which made Albert a bit sick when he looked at all that jiggling gelatin and hard-cooked eggs. He was having the corn chowder and biscuits, one of his favorites, although he didn't dine at the club often. His mother had pushed him to become a member, and he had been accepted quickly as Sir Wendell's son, even though he had been one of its youngest members at that time. He glanced up at Cousin Freddy as his words finally sank in.

"Miss Thompson? Are you referring to Miss Kirsty Thompson?"

"Ah, is that the name? Very common folk from what I've heard, with that hooligan fighter among them, although one of the sisters married into the Pendergast family. I'm sure they're regretting that." Freddy laughed. He signaled the waiter for more wine.

"You know nothing of them. You'd best not share any gossip

about Miss Thompson. I have great regard for her and am actively courting her."

Freddy laid down his silverware and frowned. "Strange that Aunt Althea has only recently been introduced to her, and not as an intimate. Why have you not been forthcoming? She was terribly disappointed at your preference, especially after she heard of your rather public display last week near State House Square."

Albert put his wineglass down rather forcefully, sloshing the contents on the starched linen cloth. He waved away a waiter coming toward their table. "What have you told her, Freddy? What did you say?"

"I'm only thinking of our family, Albert. You don't seem to anymore."

He narrowed his eyes. "Do not try and convince me to increase the annual amount Father settled on you. I won't do it. You have no employment or activities. You have a comfortable town house—owned by me, I might add. Be satisfied that I increase the amount of your income by a percentage every year to make Mother happy."

"I am a gentleman, Albert. As you should be too instead of mucking around at a hospital or in a laboratory." Freddy shivered. "All those diseases and unclean bodies."

"We're not in England, Freddy," Albert growled. "Lounging about doing nothing because of some familial good fortune is frowned upon in America. Self-made men are the standard."

Freddy shrugged and picked up his fork. Albert could not let the silence last.

"What did you tell Mother about Miss Thompson?"

"Just that she nearly climbed in your lap and kissed you in front of a crowd of onlookers on one occasion and is setting up some sort of warehouse, quite lowering, don't you think, for her to be in trade. It seems to many people that she has set her sights on a wealthy and successful man regardless of his family's feelings or objections. There is some rumor of her traveling some distance with just you and that unfortunate secretary you employ without a chaperone in sight, but I quickly put that notion to rest. Although Edith Fairchild seems certain of it, having traveled on the same ship to New York, and she seems to know everything about everyone, if one reads the society pages in the *Inquirer*! But I know you would never be involved in *that* sort of common peccadillo."

Albert willed himself to remain calm and not react in any way. Freddy was staring at him and undoubtedly was looking for some indication that it was true. "I have no idea what you're talking about, Freddy. I am respectfully courting Miss Thompson. I'm sure you've shared all of this with Mother, but be careful," he said and rose, tossing his linen napkin on the table. He signaled a waiter to him. "Please take care of Mr. Masterson and add the bill to my account." He turned back to Freddy and leaned close to his ear. "Father is gone, and I control the family money. I could cut you off without a cent, and there would be nothing you or Mother could do. Be careful how far you push."

Freddy looked up at him with all the loathing Albert knew was behind his cousin's typically gallant façade. Albert turned and walked away, his mind churning, but he knew what he must do.

"Here you are, Mother," Albert said after opening the door to the drawing room. "Do you have a moment? There is something I'd like to discuss with you."

She barely glanced at him. "I'm not feeling well. I've just told Graybell I'll have tea and some soup in my rooms."

"This won't take long." He moved an embroidery hoop and sat down in front of her on the hassock near her chair. His long legs were nearly bent double. She looked at him askance.

"Sit in a chair correctly, Albert. I've taught you better."

He shook his head. "I want to be certain we are close enough to completely understand each other."

"I can hardly imagine what is so im—"

"Don't dissemble, Mother. We are going to discuss what Cousin Freddy has told you about Miss Kirsty Thompson."

She laid her magazine in her lap and looked up at him, eyes wide, her lips pinched. "Do you mean when that woman, that tart, mauled you in public? Is that to which you refer?"

"Her name is Miss Kirsty Thompson. My behavior toward her was not acceptable, but I am hoping she will forgive me and agree to be my wife." Albert took a deep, slow breath, waiting for the shouting and other unpleasantness that was bound to ensue with this announcement.

"Strange, then, that she referred to you today as her affianced at the Library Association luncheon I attend every year. Our donation amount is on your desk to be sent with their usual paperwork. Do as you will about this woman, Albert. You've never been solicitous of your mother. You always sided with your father against me," she stood slowly, holding the armrests of her chair, and he rose too. "Good night, Albert."

He watched her hobble across the room, her hand touching the back of the settee to steady herself, then her fingers touching the writing desk near the door. To anyone watching, she was so feeble she needed to support herself for the distance from her chair near the fireplace to the door, now being opened by Graybell. He knew she was not so frail. He'd seen her hurrying from one part of the house to the other without hanging on to furniture or using a cane. It struck him then how much of her behavior was meant to affect him in some way, and he found it incredibly sad that she did not feel she could just be herself in front of him. He was her *son*.

KIRSTY SAT ON THE FLOOR, LEANING BACK AGAINST THE CHAIR in Aunt Murdoch's room, while her hair was unbraided and brushed. Time like this together with her aunt was one of her earliest memories of growing up in the Locust Street house. She had been unsettled as a child; that was as good a name as any for her behavior then, she supposed. Looking back, she was sure that her parents' murder when she was five years old had been more deeply disturbing than her childish brain's understanding of life and everyone's inevitable death could fathom. She had been terrified of being alone or left behind and often acted badly rather than admit her fears. Murdoch had saved her from punishment and from herself many times. Aunt Murdoch would lead her to her sleeping room whenever Kirsty disobeyed Muireall or James. She would sit in the large, soft chair by the window, her legs apart so Kirsty could lean back and have her hair brushed with the silver-backed brush until her hair crackled and glimmered in the light.

She closed her eyes with the first brushstroke from her forehead to the length of hair laying in Murdoch's lap, as it was waist length when down. Even the pulls on knots or tangles felt good, let alone the scratch of the bristles on her scalp, which nearly put her to sleep. She murmured her appreciation.

"Always did love getting your hair brushed and played with," Aunt said and pulled Kirsty's hair back above her ear with a long stroke. They sat in silence until Murdoch leaned down and whispered in her ear. "What is it, girl? What's troubling you?"

She folded her hands in her lap and took a moment to gather her random thoughts. "I've got to make a decision, Aunt, and I think regardless of what I choose, there's going to be unpleasantness, and maybe heartbreak. Maybe for a lifetime."

"Quite a weighty subject for you, Kirsty girl," Aunt said and huffed a laugh. "You've never been one to be melancholy or think too far ahead, not like Muireall, who rarely thinks of today, as she's planning a decade from now."

"Perhaps that is a character flaw of mine that has just surfaced." She tilted her head so the brush would get under her hair at the back of her neck.

"I don't think so, but why don't you tell me what's bothering you? You'll feel the better for it."

"Shall I marry the man I am fairly certain I am in love with and resign myself to living with his mother, a cruel woman, or walk away now before I find myself unmarriageable? I want what Elspeth has. I want what James has. I don't want to find myself like Muireall, closing in on thirty years of age and past considering a husband or even a lover. Maybe I'm just jealous."

"You're not jealous, Kirsty. You're in love with Mr. Watson, although he is as far from the type of man who I thought would catch your eye as he could possibly be."

"Why is that?"

"You're as beautiful as your mother, dear. Maybe more. I always thought some handsome prince would bow at your feet." She chuckled.

"Albert is very handsome," Kirsty said, feeling compelled to defend him. "He's the handsomest man I've ever met. And even though he's terribly tall and awfully thin, he is very manly."

"Of course he is. You love him. You want to have babies with him and kiss him when he leaves for his work and again when he comes home after a long day. You want to hold his hand and feel his arms around you," she said softly.

"Was that how it was for you, Aunt? With your husband?"

"Heavens, no," Aunt said. "Angus Murdoch was a miserable excuse for a man. I did not shed any tears when he got drunk, fell down a ravine, and broke his neck. I knew my niece and nephew, your Ma and Da, would take care of me for as long as was necessary. Your da, Chief of the Tavistons, was the best of men."

"He was." Kirsty turned her head to look at her aunt. "Then how do you know so much about how I feel about Albert?"

Aunt turned Kirsty's shoulders back and pulled the brush through her hair. "Just because I didn't marry him didn't mean I didn't love a man with all of my heart. I did. Carson Galloway took work in a shipyard to save enough to marry me, but he was killed when a pulley let loose while setting up the main mast. They told me he didn't suffer, and I prayed it was so."

"How did you come to marry your husband?"

Aunt separated her hair into three long sections and began to braid each section. "I'd no choice, girl. My father found out I was expecting Carson's baby, and he arranged for me to marry Murdoch. I had no choice really. My father told me I was to marry him. I was nineteen. What else would I have done? I was married for three weeks and lost the babe."

Tears filled Kirsty's eyes. "Dear God, Aunt. I am so sorry. I never knew."

"No one knows who's still alive. Except me and now you."

"Do you have any regrets?" she whispered.

"Yes. I regret that I did not tell Carson I would have lived in a shack or a cave, that we would make our way and our living together as a couple. I regret letting him walk away from me without marrying him. I regret not telling him I loved him in the last letter I wrote to him because I was pouting that he could not leave his work to come home and take me to the annual festival in our valley. I regret much of it."

"So you are saying that I should just marry Mr. Watson, even knowing his mother is, well, she is a horrible person who will never care for me and will most likely try to make me miserable."

Aunt harrumphed a laugh. "It's not you that needs to change, girl. It's him. He's the one who will regret it for a lifetime if he allows his mother to chase you off. Not you, dear girl. You deserve a home, whether a mud hovel or a mansion, where love lives. Just like this house. Arguments and disagreements aside, even our hotheaded James. Dunacres in the old country was full of love, and so is this house. Full, overflowing with love. You deserve the same."

"Oh, Aunt Murdoch," she said with a shaking voice. "But what if he doesn't choose me?"

Aunt kissed her temple. "Then you'll know, girl. You'll know if he is the man for you."

Kirsty pulled her aunt's weathered hand to her lips, smelling the cream she used, feeling the wrinkled skin of her palm, and the strength still held in her fingers. She kissed Aunt's knuckles and held them against her cheek. She was safe there, in her embrace, and always heard the truth from her, even when it was not what she wanted to hear.

Albert left Charter House and went directly to Locust Street. He was disturbed by his mother's reaction to his partiality and hopes for a union with Kirsty but not surprised. He was buoyed by the comments that she'd referred to him as her affianced. What was it about her? How had she become such a part of his mind, of his future, maybe even his heart? He was no cynic, which was surprising considering his mother's behavior, but he also had thought little of love or romantic entanglements. It all seemed so unscientific, unverifiable. It was just a feeling, wasn't it? How could it be proven?

But he admitted love could not be dissected and examined in the same way a cadaver or a glass under a microscope could be, nor should it be. In a very short time, her face had become the vision he dreamed of, the one he drifted off to sleep to, and the one he looked for in every other woman he saw in a crowd. He had no idea when she'd come to mean so much to him, but she did, it was a fact, even without any critical analysis. He slowed his horse in front of 75 Locust Street and jumped down from his two-seater. Maybe she'd agree to a ride in the park.

"Good afternoon, Mrs. McClintok. Is Miss Kirsty Thompson at home?" he said as he removed his hat and gloves.

"Let me see if she is at home to callers, sir. Why don't you have a seat in the parlor? You know the way, don't you?"

"I do. Thank you."

He went into the parlor, where all the Thompson family gathered, and walked over to the massive quilting hoop sitting in the rounded window with several chairs around it. There were different-colored spools of thread on the windowsill and a pin cushion with several needles sticking out of it, some with strands of thread and some without. It was a work in progress, and one that brought this family together. He was admiring the small, neat stitches when he heard a swish of skirts, but it was not whom he was expecting.

"Mr. Watson?" the old aunt said.

"Mrs. Murdoch. It is a pleasure to see you," he said and turned his hat in his hand. "Will Miss Thompson be able to join us?"

"She is considering it."

"Considering it?" he repeated and felt his unproven heart stutter.

"I am to be the chaperone, but do not worry. I'm nearly blind and deaf in one ear. I'll just sit over here and rest my eyes while we wait."

He watched her seat herself near the fireplace and get comfortable in a tufted chair. Her eyes closed immediately, and he slid onto a nearby settee to wait and wonder. It was another fifteen minutes until she appeared in the doorway, and he jumped to his feet. She was not her usual self; there was no lilt to her step or smile on her face. In fact, it looked as if she'd been crying.

He hurried to her, hands outstretched. "Miss Thompson, Kirsty. What is wrong?"

She did not take his hands. She walked to two chairs with a small table between, followed by Mrs. McClintok carrying a tea tray. The housekeeper left, and Kirsty seated herself and looked up at him.

"Would you care for tea, Albert?"

"Y-yes. Yes, I would." She picked up her cup and took a sip after handing him his. He seated himself. "Kirsty, please. Tell me what is wrong. I cannot b-bear to see you this way."

"Why are you here, Albert?"

"Is it so d-distressing when I call on you? My mother told me you said we were engaged." He smiled softly. "I was very hopeful you have been convinced to accept me."

"If I accepted you, if we married, what plans do you have for where we would live?"

Albert felt a knot forming in his chest. There was something unpleasant coming; he didn't know what it was, but he could feel the tension, or maybe just the anger, rolling off her. "I assume we'd live at Charter House. It is quite large and really very beautiful and is situated near the river. There are sixteen bedrooms, formal rooms, servants' quarters, as well as stables and carriage houses."

She looked up at him then. "And your mother has been the mistress of this house since you moved to Philadelphia."

"Well, yes. She has."

"And she intends to stay at Charter House after your marriage."

He noticed that she said "your" marriage, rather than "our" marriage. He felt things falling apart quickly, all his visions of her coming to an end. "It is her home too, Kirsty. I'm sure she will come to—"

"Do not patronize me, Albert. I may be young, but I am not insensible."

He shook his head. "My cousin, Frederick, told my mother about our kiss in the carriage last week. She was not pleased, of course, but she will come around. I'm sure of it."

"Are you sure of it, Albert? Are you? Did she tell you about the luncheon at the Philadelphia Library Association? Did she tell you see saw me attending with my sisters and sister-in-law? Did you realize it was the first time I ventured out after our kiss in the carriage? I am not afraid of social censure; however, I am aware of it and how gossip could affect us, possibly your career, and my new business, which I am telling you right now I will not forfeit upon my marriage to any man!"

She was nearly shouting now and red in the face. She stood and paced to the windows, and he could see the rise and fall of her shoulders as she took deep breaths, attempting to calm herself.

"Please, Kirsty. Tell me what has happened," he whispered.

She turned to him with tears in her eyes. "Your mother saw me with my family and shouted across a room full of guests asking how I could show my face among good Christian women."

He jumped to his feet. "Surely, surely not," he said. But he could see his mother saying just that sort of thing. He didn't want to believe it, though.

And that was when her shoulders slumped, when the color drained from her cheeks, and she covered her face with her hands. "Good day, Mr. Watson," she said as she ran from the room.

He turned quickly to follow her, but Mrs. Murdoch stopped him. "You need to hear it all. Wait here."

A few moments later, Muireall came into the room. "Mr. Watson."

"Miss Thompson," he said, his voice shaking.

"Please be seated," she said and sat down in the chair Kirsty had just vacated. He sat again in his chair.

"I will not patronize you with offers of more tea, Mr. Watson. I'm not sure what Kirsty has told you about the event at the Philadelphia Library Association luncheon, but your mother shouted at her from across the room, bringing every other voice in a room of one hundred or more women to silence. She said Kirsty was not fit to be around good Christian women."

"She has told me that. I know my mother can be unpleasant, but it's hard to imagine—"

"She referred to Kirsty as a tramp who had molested her son and was seen pawing at his person. Kirsty turned to the door as your mother continued shouting, but she stopped and walked directly to Lady Watson. Kirsty told her she was bringing shame on her own son, and what a fine and brilliant man you were. She took responsibility for that public display of affection but said it was because the two of you were affianced and occasionally such couples are less than proper. Your mother shrieked at that and claimed you were a gentleman and would never join yourself to a woman who was lost to all good behavior. I was terribly proud of Kirsty as she continued to speak in moderate tones and mildly chided your mother for embarrassing you with her behavior, especially as it was a room full of Philadelphia society women, sure to go to their respective homes and churches and repeat every word that was said. At that point, I asked your mother to join us for the engagement festivities, as did my sister-in-law, Mrs. Thompson. Kirsty conducted herself as a lady with decorum but was visibly shaken by your mother's diatribe. I have told her she should marry you considering all this public history between the two of you, but I will support her in whatever she chooses to do. Now," she stood, "I have kept you too long, Mr. Watson. I'm sure you are in a hurry to leave."

Albert stood, not sure his legs would hold him, feeling as if he were in a cloud, that all his thoughts were murky and unclear. He bowed, an automatic and outdated reaction, and hurried to the door. *Dear Lord. What must she think of me?*

# CHAPTER 12

"What do you think, James?" Kirsty asked as they walked through the narrow warehouse she was looking at for storing her imported fabrics.

"It needs a good cleaning, but that's nothing you and the rest of the family can't handle. I'm thinking we should build a wall right here, with a door, so that you can have a showroom. Put some windows in the front and you're selling to tailors and seamstresses in their shops *and* to shoppers walking by. You're only a little away from all the other shops in this neighborhood."

"I was thinking the same thing. I don't want to be foolish, though. Would it be expensive to build the wall?"

James put his hands on his hips and turned around. He shook his head. "MacAvoy and I can do it, but you'll have to hire a mason to enlarge those windows and a glazier to fill them. You and Elspeth and Muireall can paint it in one day."

"What about me?" Lucinda said as she walked to them. "I can help."

"I don't want you smelling those fumes," he said and dropped his voice. "Not in your condition."

Lucinda smiled. "Maybe we'll have open windows by then and won't have to worry about the smell—or my *condition*."

James reached an arm out and snaked it around Lucinda's waist, bringing her against him, hip to shoulder. "Have you ever painted a thing in your life?" he asked with a smile, looking down into her upturned face.

"No, but I can learn. You've said I'm a fast learner," Lucinda replied with a slow blink of her eyelids and a knowing smile.

Her husband growled. "That's not what I was talking about, woman."

Kirsty turned away from the intimacy between them. She had to. She'd been miserable for the two weeks since she'd last spoken to Albert. He had called on her many times, but she refused to receive him, hurrying to her room or to the kitchens. She was convinced the only cure for the heartache she felt was to make a clean break from him. Remove him from her presence and her mind, she thought as the door to the warehouse opened.

"Mr. Cartwright?"

The man pulled his hat from his head and smiled. "Miss Thompson. Looking lovely as usual."

"How did you know I was here?" she asked, feeling gooseflesh rise on her neck.

James walked over. "Cartwright? My father-in-law, Mr. Vermeal, told me he'd introduced you to my sister. I don't imagine he told you about this location."

Cartwright shook his head and shrugged. "He didn't. I just happen to know most of the rental agents in the city. One of them told me a young woman was looking to open a warehouse for imported wools and yarn at this location. I thought it had to be you."

Kirsty didn't trust this man, but she did respect that he was knowledgeable and experienced. What could it possibly hurt to ask his opinion? "What do you think of this location, Mr. Cartwright?"

Cartwright smiled. "I'd be happy to offer you my opinion after I've seen the entire property. Would you give me a tour, Miss Thompson?"

"I suppose I could do that," she said and curled her hand around his outstretched arm. James watched her and lined himself up on Cartwright's other side. She was right on both counts, though. Donald Cartwright was very helpful concerning the shelving that would have to be built to store the rolls of fabric and skeins of yarn, but she did not believe he was honest, or even forthcoming.

"Have you received your copy of the contract from us?" he asked after their tour had been completed and they had stepped out onto the street.

"I forwarded it to Mr. Vermeal for review; however, he has said we will not sign that copy. We will wait for a new contract to be written after the changes we have requested have been added or removed, and then we will read it again with you both present and sign if everything is to our satisfaction."

"Well," Cartwright smiled broadly, "aren't you the accomplished lady of business?"

"I don't believe you are complimenting me. Perhaps I should look into another shipper."

"No need to be hasty, Kirsty. I may call you Kirsty, shan't I?"

"No," James said coolly. "She is Miss Thompson to you."

"No need to get angry, Thompson," Cartwright said. "I am, after all, just trying to help."

"And we thank you sincerely for your advice," she said. "I must return the keys to the rental agent soon. Good day, Mr. Cartwright."

He stared at her for a long minute and then put his hat on his head and tapped it into place. "It's been a pleasure, Miss Thompson," he said and turned to James with a nod. "Thompson."

That was when she noticed Albert Watson standing a few feet away, staring at her and twirling his hat in his hands.

"Miss Thompson," he said quietly. "May I speak to you?"

She gasped, and had she not caught herself, she would have hurried to him to hold his hands in hers. He looked dreadful, and she wondered if he'd been ill. There were dark circles under his eyes, and his cheeks were pale.

James glanced at her. "Kirsty?" he asked softly.

She looked at her brother. "Can you wait a few moments in your carriage?"

He gave Albert a sharp look. "For a few minutes."

Kirsty waited until he was in the carriage with his wife and took a few steps closer to Albert, although not as close as her heart would have preferred, but her head prevailed.

"You do not look well, Albert. Have you been ill?"

He shook his head. "Just," he said and stopped to clear his throat. "Just not sleeping well."

"Your clothes are hanging on you. Have you not been eating properly?"

"Not much appetite, but that is not why I wanted to talk to you."

"What is it, then? Why do you want to talk to me?"

"I can't understand why you are refusing to see me. I thought we h-had come to an understanding. I miss you dreadfully, and I know you were embarrassed when we were in the carriage b-but . . ."

"Please do not make yourself upset," she said, her voice quivering. "I think it is for the best that we end our acquaintance. I think we will only cause each other heartache."

He took one step closer to her. "Why did you run out of the room that day? Why did you not tell me yourself what happened with mother? Why leave it to your sister? Have I meant so little to you?"

"You mean very much to me, Albert. You must believe me."

"Then why?"

"Because at some point you will have to choose. You'll have to choose between your mother and your wife, and I am not sure you would choose me. Do you remember what you said when I told you what Lady Watson said to me at the luncheon? Do you?"

He shook his head and swallowed. "I'm not sure. You were looking so upset."

"I told you that she shouted across the room asking how I could show my face among good Christian women," she said, beginning to be as angry as she was upset. "And then you said surely not. That was when I realized what our life would be like. You would be defending your mother to me and me to your mother for the rest of our lives. I don't want that. I want a house full of love, which I have enjoyed all my life, in Scotland as a very young child and on Locust Street. Why would I purposefully put myself in the power of a person who is so unhappy?"

ALBERT SWALLOWED. HE DID NOT KNOW WHAT TO SAY; IT WAS the only life he'd ever known other than the time spent with his father. Perhaps there really was nothing to say and he was destined to live a lonely life with an unhappy woman. But maybe Kirsty was taking this all too seriously.

"Mother sometimes says outrageous things. I ignore most of it."

"Of course you do. You go to work and do not concern yourself with the management of the household—cleaning, meals, staff. You are not involved, as a wife would be, with any of this. A wife would be subject to her cruelty."

"But can you not just disregard her? Everyone does except a few persons who wish to ingratiate themselves with her."

"No, I cannot. Every meal would be tense. Every holiday unhappy. And you must face facts. It is very possible she will refuse to have anything to do with me and tell everyone she meets whatever she determines is true. I'm not concerned with gossip, but I am not impervious to it either."

"You seemed able to manage her the first time you met her, g-guiding her to sit down and introducing her to your family."

"That was before I knew what she was capable of, and I fear it will be worse if we press forward with an engagement."

"Is there nothing I c-can do?"

She shook her head slowly, and tears filled her eyes. "I love you, Albert. I am sure of it. But I don't think I can give up the idea of family love for you. I was raised with sisters and brothers and an aunt and cousins who love me and whom I love. I don't want to live any other way. I'm so sorry. Please take care of yourself."

He watched her turn and hurry to her brother's carriage. He was numb with the thought that she loved him. He could not make his legs move, although he reached for her, knowing she was gone, that he would not touch her again. The carriage did not move. The door flew open, and James Thompson jumped down onto the cobblestones and walked straight to him, stopping when he was but inches from Albert.

"You dumb son of a bitch," Thompson hissed and pointed to the carriage. "You have managed to make the happiest girl in the world unbearably sad, and I won't stand for it. I don't know all the details, nor do I want to. I will tell you that my wife's father hates me, and I have little use for him. She would never make me live with him and endure his snobbery every single day, although he has settled somewhat since he found out his daughter is expecting my child. But that's what marriage is. Choosing. Marriage is *choosing* who will be at your side. Lucinda chose me, and I chose her. If you've chosen Kirsty, then fight for her. Do something. If you've chosen your current life, then do us all a favor and never darken her door again. You're breaking her heart."

Albert gulped down the sudden lump in his throat as he watched Thompson climb into his carriage. Choose his current life? Life with his mother and no chance at being with the woman he loved? Because he surely loved Kirsty Thompson. He wanted her, all of her. He wanted to know her mind, and he wanted to know her hopes and dreams, and he wanted her naked body against his. This was love. It had to be. And he was breaking her heart.

Albert went home to Charter House, looking at the grand building as he approached, remembering how he'd felt when he purchased it. The pride and the happiness in this expansive, well-built, and beautiful home still lingered, but it could not define him. It was brick and mortar, not soft hands and warm kisses.

He went inside to his training room and pulled on loose pants and a shirt. He spent some of his time there nearly every day, lifting his weights, stretching his muscles, and punching the leather bag that hung from the ceiling by a chain. He could think in that room; doing those exercises, he could let his mind drift while his body ached and sweat poured down his back. It was freeing and gave him ample time to decide. To perhaps take Thompson's advice and choose. But he could not convince himself that his mother wasn't mostly innocuous since she lived much of her life in two rooms, greeting few guests and visiting less.

"Oh. I'm sorry to interrupt, sir," Clyde Clawson said. "I'll come back another time."

"No, please feel free to stay. I am nearly done. Have you been using the weights frequently?"

"Yes, often." Clawson smiled. "I believe it is helping me gain lost strength, although it makes the scars a bit uncomfortable. Mrs. Munchin gave me a salve that has helped."

"I rarely meet you here. When do you usually come?"

Clawson's face colored. "I often come when the house is abed."

"If you're worried what the staff will think, don't. I made it clear to Graybell that you would be accessing this room and doing your exercises."

"Thank you, sir," he said and glanced away from Albert.

"What is it, Clawson?"

"Nothing, sir. I just prefer to come to this area of the house when I'm least likely to disturb the family."

Albert stared at him. "Disturb the family? My rooms are . . ." he trailed off. "Is it Mother? You do not wish to disturb my mother?"

Clawson nodded, although he still would not look him in the eye. "Yes. I wouldn't want to disturb Lady Watson."

In the past, he would have dismissed outright any concerns or hints that his mother caused any disturbances more than a minor upset. He wondered now if he'd grossly underestimated her impact on those in her sphere.

"What has happened, Clawson?"

The young man said nothing at first, just shifting from one foot to the other. "I really enjoy my job, sir. I'm certain that many would never give me a chance because of what I look like or where I came from. I'm able to send quite a bit of my salary to my mother every week because of my living arrangements. I'm very grateful, sir."

Albert sat down on the wide bench in the middle of the room. "Tell me, Clyde. What has she said to you?"

"Lady Watson has some concerns that I am stealing from the household," he said, his head bent to his chest. He looked up quickly. "I would never, sir. I would never betray the great trust you've put in me."

"I know that. Remember that I employ you, not my mother. I'm the only one who can offer or rescind employment. What else did she say?"

"She says it is upsetting to her to see my deformities. I do my best to stay out of her vision."

Albert stood and went to the young man. "You are not deformed, Clyde. You were burned horribly in a heroic attempt to save your sister. Those scars are honorable. You must not listen to my mother."

He nodded. "I know. But it is hard, sir. She is the mistress of the house."

"She is," he said. "But that does not give her the right to insult you. You must tell me if you have more unpleasant interactions with her or with anyone else here. This is your employment, but it is also your home, Clyde."

"Thank you, sir."

Albert left the room and went straight to his bathing room. He would soak and he would think. Apparently, Miss Thompson was not the only person who was affected by his mother. He could tell Clawson was troubled and most likely frightened by his mother's treatment of him and by her comments. Had she threatened his employment? Most likely she had.

Could he allow Kirsty Thompson to walk away? It had already happened, and he'd not even understood why. But she'd said she loved him, and he allowed himself to be deliriously happy long enough to slide down in the tub, dunk his whole head, and come up shaking his hair like a dog with a wet coat. He smiled with the thought of it. She loved him. He'd never anticipated or dreamed or even desired the undefinable emotion of romantic love, but he was now its recipient. There was a reason poets wrote about love and empires rose and fell with the gain or loss of it.

But it was only a few short moments until he realized none of that mattered. She'd removed herself from his life. And more so, how could he honor his mother when it appeared she was the least honorable of his acquaintances? He could not in good conscience be dismissive of her or be less than gentlemanly. His father always managed it, and he must endeavor to do so as well. But would he allow her to ruin his life, darken the love he felt for Kirsty Thompson? He didn't think he could. He would have to do something to separate her from the people in his life.

. . .

## THE PROFESSOR'S LADY

Kirsty knew she shouldn't go anywhere alone. She knew it and did it anyway. She was feeling lost and lonely and thoroughly unhappy. She climbed into the streetcar that would take her to the site of her shop. She'd met with Mr. Vermeal, Donald Cartwright, and Pierre Arnaud and signed the contracts a few days prior. She'd barely been able to breathe as she signed her name, only glancing at Mr. Vermeal for encouragement, who met her eyes and nodded once.

But today she slipped out the kitchen door, up the stone steps, away from the men guarding the Locust Street house, and traveled alone to the site. She leaned close to the open window of the streetcar, holding the leather strap, feeling the rumble of the cobblestones against the wheels, and letting the cool air wash over her.

She was seriously considering stopping the work being done on the shop space and giving James, Muireall, and Elspeth back their stakes in the business. Mr. Vermeal was also interested in investing, but she'd told him she felt she had enough to begin, to get the storefront ready and order the wools she needed for an inventory, although the cost of the order had nearly taken her breath away when she'd telegraphed it to her contact in Scotland. Could she cancel the order?

She would move to another city. Maybe Baltimore, not so far from Philadelphia and her nephew, but a new town nonetheless. She had enough saved from her share of their family's canning business to live modestly for a full year, she calculated, to try and figure out what was next for her and mostly put considerable distance between her and Mr. Albert Watson.

Kirsty took a deep breath. Even hearing his name in the privacy of her own thoughts was enough to stir the longing she felt in the pit of her stomach from a banked flicker to a roaring flame. The streetcar slowed, and she stepped down and hurried toward her shop. *Her shop.* It would be hard to leave this physical manifestation of her dreams. She straightened her shoulders and stamped her foot. She refused, absolutely refused, to leave everything behind, everything and everyone she loved and held dear, because of Albert Watson.

She glanced left and right and slipped the key into the lock to open the door. The enlarged windows were complete, filling the front of the shop with light. She closed and relocked the door and lit the lamp hanging on the wall before stepping through the doorless opening to the backroom. James and MacAvoy had built the wall and ordered a wide door to accommodate the space, but the woodworker had not delivered it yet. The paint she'd chosen sat in the corner, waiting for her and her sisters to do the painting, and the massive countertop and the base it would sit on, for the front of the shop, were stacked against the wall.

She turned a slow circle, looking through the opening to the front of the store, and saw the knob on the door jiggle as if someone were trying to get in.

ALBERT STOOD IN THE HALL OUTSIDE OF HIS MOTHER'S PARLOR and took a deep breath. He was going to tell her that he would be moving out of Charter House and into a house near Alexander's home. It was no palatial mansion, but it was not tiny either and would be a small stretch on his finances unless he began to insist that Frederick pay rent on the townhome he lived in, which he seriously thought he would do.

The grounds were not a quarter the size of his current home, but it had seven bedrooms, accommodations for staff, including an apartment over the carriage house, which he thought would suit Mr. Clawson. The kitchens were modern, and there were bathing rooms for the master suite and public rooms for entertaining on the first floor. He thought at that moment how pitiful it was that his elderly mother would be alone, but for servants, in this massive, cold house, but he would not be deterred. He stepped up to the door and heard his mother's voice.

"Why do you think nothing will come of it, Frederick? That hussy has her claws in him!"

Albert stepped close and put his ear to the door. He saw Graybell at the end of the hall, motioning to him.

"What?" he whispered.

"You can hear better from the servants' door, sir."

Albert hurried behind the butler until he'd gone through the concealed door, a few steps down a narrow hall, stopping where the man indicated. Graybell continued on, and Albert bent down and looked through the keyhole. The butler was right. Albert could see and hear everything.

"It will all be over then," Freddy said. "Trust me, Aunt."

"And you believe this man is to be trusted?"

"I do. I need an additional one thousand dollars to satisfy our bargain, and then our problems will be solved."

"Once *she* is no longer influencing him, my son, my Albert, will come to his senses and treat me as I deserve. I am his mother, after all."

"You're so right, Aunt. Let me help you regain your rightful place in his life, and perhaps, when he comes to his senses, he will see fit to reward me, his humble cousin, your dear brother's only son."

"Of course, Freddy. You're the nephew of a baron and so should be treated with dignity."

"Well, Aunt, I must be away to meet this man and give him the final amount as he has already turned the key over to those other men and he is not the type of man one should keep waiting. He told me they have been watching her home, so they will know when she slips away, and if luck is with us, she will visit her little shop, if she does not, they will just pull down some shelving or break some windows in her storefront. She will undoubtedly be frightened enough if she is at her shop, and maybe even ruined, to never bother our dear Albert again."

A shiver trailed down Albert's back. His mind was slow when

contemplating something evil. It was so far from the norm in his thoughts, other than what he read in the occasional medical records of the previous centuries. But this . . . this was wicked, he knew it, whatever the plot's details entailed.

He opened the hidden door and stepped into the room.

"We need nothing, Graybell," his mother said.

"It is not Graybell, Mother."

She turned in her desk chair, and Freddy looked up from where he leaned over her as she wrote. "Whatever are you doing in the servants' hallway, Albert?"

His mother did not blink, look away, or in any way indicate she may have been involved with something dastardly, but Cousin Freddy was a different story. His eyes drifted from Albert's, and he edged toward the door of the room.

"Not so fast, Freddy!" Albert shouted and bolted across the carpet, grabbing his cousin's arm and whirling him to face him.

"What have you done? Who are you paying?"

Freddy's eyes darted to his mother. He licked his lips. "I don't know what you're talking about, Cousin."

Albert lifted him by his shirtfront and pressed him back against the wall. His mother was shouting in the background, and he turned his head. "Quiet!"

She dropped into her chair, silent and wide-eyed.

"You will tell me everything," he said softly, just inches from Freddy's face. "A key to what and to whom is it being given. Tell me it all now or . . ."

"Or what, Albert?" Freddy asked with raised brows. "Or what?"

"Or you will be cut off without a cent. You will lose your home and your income, although you may lose it anyway if I find out you have endangered her."

"I don't know whom you're speaking of," Freddy said.

"Put him down this instant," his mother shouted.

Albert released him and let him drop to the floor in a heap. "What have you two done? Tell me now."

"It's your own fault, Albert. Traipsing around in the gutter with that hussy. I told you I'd be happy to instruct a young *lady* in the household—"

"I don't care what you think about her, Mother. I want to know right now why you are writing a check to Freddy and what the key opens," he said very softly but with a gaze of steely determination. Freddy pushed himself up from the floor, but Albert pushed him back with his foot, holding him there by the neck. "Right now. *Tell me right now.*"

His mother's eyes were wide, and the color drained from her face. "This sort of violence is hardly necessary."

"I'll determine that, Mother." He pressed on Freddy's neck until he whimpered. "The check and the key. Tell me now."

"There's a man who has the key to her shop," Freddy croaked.

"Who? Who's the man?"

"Cartwright. His name is Cartwright," his mother said. "There'll be no harm done to her, of course. Just some others who will break a window or pull down some shelving. Enough to frighten her from her ridiculous notions and away from you permanently."

"Why would she be frightened of me?" he asked. His mother looked away, and he pressed his heel on Freddy's neck.

"They . . . they are to tell her that you paid them to do it."

"She'd never believe them. When is this to happen? What day?" he shouted.

"You're too late," his mother said. "Cartwright has already given the men the key."

"Today?"

"Perhaps. They've been watching her house to see when she leaves."

"We've already paid Cartwright half. This check will be the final payment. Now let Freddy off of the floor so he can deliver it and we can get our lives back to normal, the way it was before any of us knew the name Thompson!" his mother screamed and waved the paper in the air.

He pulled Freddy off the floor, dragging him to the door. "You will tell me where you are to meet him. Take me there."

"I want no parts of any violence," Freddy said as he rubbed his neck.

Albert leaned close. "Too late, Cousin." He pulled a sheet of vellum from the drawer of his mother's desk as she looked on. He penned the note after Freddy told him the location, sealed it in an envelope, and handed it to him. "Instead, take this to James Thompson at the Thompson Sporting Arena. If he is not there, go to 75 Locust Street and hand it to Miss Thompson, Miss Muireall Thompson. If I find that you have not done exactly as I've told you, I will hunt you down and no one will ever find your body. Do you understand me?"

"Albert!" his mother shouted.

But Freddy just looked into Albert's eyes and then took the envelope in his shaking hand. "I'll deliver it immediately."

"Then make yourself scarce while I make decisions regarding this family's benevolence."

# CHAPTER 13

Kirsty watched the knob move and heard the slide of the key in the lock. No one knew where she was or even that she'd left the house. Did they? If they took her as they'd taken Elspeth, her life would be over. Was she prepared to die? Did she have those regrets that Murdoch had? She thought she might. But she wasn't ready to go down without a fight. She blew out her lamp and went to the back entrance, hoping to sneak out before she was found, but she saw a shadow pass by the gap in the door. There was someone waiting in the alley!

Kirsty hurried to the trapdoor in the back of the warehouse. She lifted the heavy door by the iron ring and pulled it back into place as she went down the stone steps and onto the dirt floor. There was a bit of light filtering through the filthy window, and she could see now that the room was filled with old boxes and crates and some broken furniture.

She refused to listen to the scurrying of rodents running along the wall. She pulled a broken desk under the window, hiked up her skirts, and climbed up. She rubbed a clean spot on the window with the sleeve of her jacket and peered outside. She was level with the alley behind her shop and could see piled crates and rubbish against the opposite side. She could also see a man's legs and boots come into view as he paced close to her in front of her grimy window. She had no angle to see who he was, but she could hear him speak to another man.

"What did you do with him?"

"In the breezeway. We'll be long gone before they find him. What a bit of luck she decided to venture out today. Where is she?"

The men walked away from the window, and she could no longer hear them, but there was little doubt the "she" he spoke of was her. She dropped down to the dirt floor and fell to her knees, knowing that James's accusations about her rash behavior were true. All of it. Again. She was in danger and would cause her family heartache when they found her body. She gulped. She only hoped she would not disgrace herself with tears or begging, that she would be able to be brave to the end.

She remembered the stories of her mother after Payden had been kidnapped as an infant and her return on foot with him after his rescue, to the Taviston castle, Dunacres, running through woods and across fields, holding him against her breast with one hand and wielding a battle sword with the other. Kirsty went to the pile of rubble in the back of the cellar and began to remove boxes and crates from the pile, looking for a weapon.

"Aha," she whispered and pulled a cargo hook from between the junk. It was heavy metal with a wooden handle, black with grime. The hook was the length of her forearm, with a flat end that was spiked. She could hurt someone with that, she thought. She heard a thump near the window, pulled herself up on the rickety desk, and peered through the clean spot on the glass.

"Oh dear Lord," she said as she watched Albert Watson in the middle of the alley swing his arm hard and fast, his hair flying, and his fist slamming into the face of another man. The other man went down, and Albert straightened, heaved a breath, and looked the building up and down. Kirsty pounded on the window and screamed his name. He ran her direction and dropped to his knees.

"Get away from the window," he shouted. She clamored off the desk and backed away quickly, covering her face with her hands as Albert kicked in the window. He stuck his head inside. "Take off your petticoats. I think you can fit through this window."

She glanced up at him, sweat running down his face, blood trickling from one side of his mouth, his hand outstretched to her, giving her direction as if he was fully in charge of this dangerous situation.

Kirsty pulled up her dress and unfastened her petticoat, letting it fall to the dirt floor. She picked it up and climbed back onto the desk, pushing the hook and the garment through the window. Albert used the petticoat to clear the broken glass from the window frame but stopped suddenly.

"I hear someone coming," he said and reached his hands through the opening.

She looked at the ceiling above her and felt the rumble of boots on boards. She wrapped her hands around his elbows, and he pulled her through, barely getting her hips through the opening. He gave one final pull, and she landed facedown in the garbage strewn along the edge of the building. Albert jumped to his feet and grabbed her hand. "Hurry, Kirsty. We haven't much—"

"There she is!"

A man grabbed her around the waist, and she screamed and kicked as he began dragging her down the alley. She fought, twisting and turning in the man's arms, glancing at Albert, now being held by a rough character while another one pummeled his stomach and face.

"Albert!"

He lifted his head to see her and kicked out at his assailant with both long legs, bringing him and the man holding him to the ground. He jumped up and kicked the downed man, facing off with the last one, his fists raised.

"Albert won't be helping you! He's who sent us! You're just too much bother and too loose for him!" He whispered in her ear and cackled a laugh. "But never you mind. We solved his problem, and you'll solve ours when your family gives up the boy." He wrapped an arm around her neck, stilling her.

And then the door from the building opened and two more men came out, one wielding a pistol. She bit down hard on the bare skin between her captor's filthy sleeve and his hand. He pulled her away from his body with one arm and cuffed her on the temple with the closed fist of his other. Her eyes rolled back in her head.

"KIRSTY! STAY STRONG," ALBERT SHOUTED AND SPIT BLOOD. That was when the door from the building opened, and two more men ran into the alley. They grabbed the man who'd been holding Kirsty and started to flee with her. He knew he was overwhelmed, but he had no intention of going down without a fight. He would save her—he must!

"Kirsty!" he heard from the open end of the alley. He turned to the shout as a man near him raised his arm and fired a gun.

He saw Alexander Pendergast drop to his knees and heard James Thompson shout—a charge so visceral, so animal-like, that a cold shiver trailed down his arms even as sweat poured off him. All of them looked at Thompson as he ran at them full bore, including the man who was busy aiming at James. Albert charged the man, slamming into the arm holding the gun, making the bullet go wide into the back of a brick building. Two more men joined the fray, jumping down from the carriage sitting at the end of the alley, heading straight for Kirsty, who was lying limp on the ground.

Albert got to her first and picked her up in his arms, turning away from the two now chasing him, running through the scrum of men. He passed Pendergast pummeling a man even as blood ran down his arm from his shoulder. Thompson was fighting two and winning and screamed as Albert went by.

"Get her out of here, Watson. Go!"

Albert didn't look back, running full speed, not thinking about how exhausted he was and how Kirsty bobbed about in his arms like a rag doll. He ran headlong into MacAvoy, the Thompson family friend, nearly as tall as he.

"Where is James?" he shouted.

"Down the alley. Six against him and Pendergast, who has been shot."

MacAvoy grinned. "Ah. Should be a quick fight, then. Go. Get her out of here."

Albert grunted as he nearly tripped and fell. He looked down and saw the slack and very dead eyes of the fellow Kirsty had danced with that evening at the Vermeal ball. Cartwright. Cartwright was his name, he knew now. He stepped over the body and set off at a run again.

Albert rounded the corner out of the alley, saw his two-seat buggy, and hoisted her onto the seat, climbing up beside her and pulling her against him, yawing his horse to move. He set a brisk pace, but once clear of the block, he slowed down since he did not want to draw attention to himself or to her. He took a long route around the city, watching to see if anyone was following him, but as he rode up and down quiet, tree-lined streets in a neighborhood of homes, he decided it was time to get to his destination and see to her injuries.

Albert rounded the next corner, turned into an alley, pulled the buggy into a small carriage house, and quickly slid the doors closed behind it. He pulled the harnesses from his horse and led him to a stall, where there was fresh hay and a bucket of water, all of which he'd done early that morning in preparation for his move to this new house. He pulled the key from his pocket, picked up

Kirsty, and went up the steps behind the stalls leading to the apartment he'd planned for Clawson. The house itself was virtually empty of all furniture and fixtures, but this apartment had been used by a retainer to watch the property until a month ago. He'd planned on telling Clawson they would replace all the furniture when he did that work on the main house, but in the meantime it was furnished, and the retainer had left nearly everything behind in the cupboards, saying the belongings were not his and he wasn't taking them. Watson was extremely happy at that moment to not have to find a way to get to a market for what he needed.

But most importantly, no one would know he was here. The agent who'd finalized the dealings for the owner was on his way with the documents to Boston, as he'd been required to deliver the paperwork in person. There was literally no one who knew where he was and, more importantly, no one who knew where Kirsty Thompson was. She moaned as he laid her down on the bed.

It just now struck him how weak he was. Whatever secretion that was in a person's body that made them able to accomplish normally undoable tasks was wearing off. He was suddenly exhausted. But he knew he must tend to her and to his own injuries, as he did not know if the threat was over or if he'd be running down yet another street with her in his arms.

The pump in the sink still worked, and he boiled water after getting a blaze going for the stovetop. He found clean sheets in a cupboard and tore them into serviceable rags, all the while checking on her every few moments, brushing the hair from her face, listening to her breathing and checking her heartbeat. He pulled his shirt over his head and washed himself, including the cuts on his face and his lip that was swollen twice its normal size. He had cuts and abrasions up and down his arms, but the most painful part of his body was his knuckles. Thompson had him boxing with padded gloves, never hitting a man's jaw or chest with his bare fist, so it was no wonder that his fingers were a mass of cuts and one was missing a portion of its fingernail. He was fairly certain that the middle finger of his right hand was broken. He wrapped it tightly against the next finger after cleaning his hands and applying some ointment he found on an upper shelf.

He filled a basin with the boiled water and went to the bedroom. Her clothing was filthy, and one side of her skirts was very bloody. He managed to get her dress off and her corset too. Why women wore the things, he did not understand as they severely limited one's breathing. But he unlaced hers, feeling not the least bit uncomfortable. She was his patient at that moment, and she needed attendance by a doctor. Him. He would attend her. He bathed her arms, her silky arms, glistening with water and the soap he'd found. He dabbed the dirt from her chest and face, lightly touching the knot on her temple that was surely the cause of her lack of consciousness. He unlaced her half boots and pulled her stockings down her legs.

The sight of one long shapely leg was enough to make him groan. This was a husband's privilege, to see his wife in such a state of undress. But a doctor too saw women's bodies as they attended them, just as he was doing now, but it did not feel professional. It felt possessive.

He exposed the other leg and saw her ripped stocking, badly torn knee, and a long cut on her thigh that was bleeding heavily. It would need stitching, and he was going to need some supplies, but it would have to wait until she was awake. He would not have her wake in a strange house alone. He wrapped her thigh tightly, hoping to stem the blood loss.

Just then she moaned and pulled her leg away as he touched a stone lodged under her skin. Her eyes fluttered open, and she looked up at him.

"Albert," she whispered. "You came for me."

He nodded. "I will always come for you, dearest."

Her eyes filled with tears. "What I have done? I've endangered everyone! Alexander," she said on an intake of breath. "He was shot! I have caused my family heartache and worry and now injury."

"When I went past him, he was fighting with both arms, although I could see some blood and his jacket was torn. I'm guessing he was grazed by the bullet, although I don't know for certain. MacAvoy arrived just as I ran away with you. He was certain they would defeat those men."

"How . . . how did you know?"

He shook his head. "I will tell you all, but first I must get a note to Clawson. You will be alone, but—"

"Albert! Your face is cut, and your hands too," she said and tried to sit up, wincing in pain and touching the side of her head.

"Careful. You must lie still. I have to get a message to Clawson and should only be gone three quarters of an hour."

She glanced around the room. "Where are we, Albert? Are we still near my warehouse?"

"We are not," he said and glanced down at his hands holding hers. "I have purchased a house for myself not far from your sister Elspeth's home. We are in the carriage house."

"You have purchased another home?" she whispered.

"I have."

"Will your mother," she cleared her throat, "will your mother be moving here with you?"

He shook his head and looked into her eyes, hopeful and beautiful. "No. She will not."

Her lip trembled. "Who will keep house for you?"

"I'm hoping to convince the woman I-I l-love to forgive me so we can be m-married."

She stared up at him and then looked away. "What do you have to tell Clawson?"

"He'll be at the c-coffeehouse he frequents, and hopefully I'll catch him. I'm going to tell him to get word to your family that you are safe and that we are going to stay hidden for a day before venturing back to Locust Street."

"Elspeth is near? We could go there."

"With a new child in residence? I won't bring t-trouble to her doorstep."

She looked up at him and lifted a hand to his cheek. "You could not have anticipated the trouble that would meet you when we met on the *Maybelle*. You must regret much of it."

"I r-regret none of it; however, I am not fond of other men hitting me with their closed fists. I am extremely grateful your brother took the time to teach me a bit about defending myself." He turned his face in her hand and kissed her palm. He felt his face redden with the gesture. "I am entirely too f-forward when I'm around you."

Kirsty smiled, and then her eyes fluttered. "I'm so tired."

He kissed her cheek and checked the bandage around her leg one more time. A spot of blood was already leaking through.

ALBERT FOUND A DARK COAT HANGING IN THE SMALL TACK room near the stalls. It was short in the sleeves but would cover up his bloody shirt sufficiently. There was a battered flat cap beside it, and he pulled it on tight, hoping the brim covered a few of the abrasions on his face. He was hoping he'd not be seen and was thankful the sun was beginning to set.

Albert hurried down the street, walking close to a group of workmen from a nearby home under construction, climbing on the streetcar behind them. Fifteen minutes later, close to the university, he stepped off near the Cap Tavern, where he knew Clawson took many of his meals with other students or assistants. He breathed a sigh of relief when he saw him in the corner with a few younger men, eating his dinner. Albert walked by, bumping Clawson as he went and dropping a note into his lap. Albert kept going straight out the door leading to the alley, where kitchen garbage was piled and a man stood with his back to him, relieving himself in a corner. He walked to the end of the alley and waited.

Clawson came through the back door, note in hand, looking right and left. Albert hissed, and Clawson hurried to him.

"Mr. Watson, I heard there was a commotion at the Charter House this morning. Are you well? You are bleeding!"

"I wish I had time to explain it all, but I don't other than to say Miss Thompson is in danger and has been hurt."

Clawson sobered immediately. "What do you need, sir?"

"I need you to go to Joseph Mosso's apothecary, you know the one, don't you? Get me laudanum, the ointment used for burns, bandages, thread and needle suitable for sewing up a cut, and anything else you think I may need. We'll need some food in the morning as well. I have very little money on me, but—"

"Never think of it, Mr. Watson. I have money. Where shall I take the items?"

"That is appreciated, Clawson. I will return the amount to you when this is over. When you have gathered what I need, go to Claremont Street and walk up and down the north side of it. I'll find you there in . . ." Albert looked at his timepiece, now covered in blood. "In one hour."

"Yes, sir."

"Be very careful you are not followed. If you must be late to lose a man, be late. Later tonight, after full dark, please go to James Thompson's home and tell him, only he or his wife, that she is safe. Use the servants' entrance. Do you know where he lives?" Albert waited for Clawson's nod. "I've got to go now. Thank you."

"Anything for Miss Thompson. She is a most wonderful lady."

Albert nodded. "She is. Now go back inside and make some excuse for why you must leave."

Clawson turned, ran to the back door, and slowed his step as he walked into the building. Albert thought morosely that he'd taught this young man more subterfuge than was healthy.

# THE PROFESSOR'S LADY

. . .

Albert hitched a ride with a produce seller heading out of the city at the end of his day and going his direction. He rode in the back of the wagon with the man's young son and sat with his hat pulled down tight, watching the streets for men he'd recognize from today's fight or from the train ride from New York, but he saw nothing out of the ordinary for a Saturday evening. He tossed the boy a penny and jumped off the back of the wagon near the street of his new home.

He hurried down his alley, after watching the neighborhood for suspicious characters, let himself in the carriage house, and turned the key in the door at the top of the steps. All was quiet, and for one moment he panicked. What if she was gone or . . . had passed away? He could not even think the word "dead." Albert hurried to the bedroom. She woke up as he looked at the bandage on her leg, soaked red. A main vein had not been severed, but still, the cut was deep and the possibility of infection was high, as the injury had undoubtedly occurred in the garbage-strewn alley behind her shop.

Albert looked out the side window of the carriage house every few minutes and saw a man walk by in the narrow view he had of the cross street at the end of his alley. He locked the door and hurried toward the street ahead. He waited at the corner of a shed until Clawson walked by and then hissed. Clawson continued walking and then turned, peering at house numbers as if he were lost. He walked toward Albert, set the paper bag on the ground, and walked away.

Albert watched Clawson walk down the street, picked up the bag, and hurried back to his carriage house. He boiled water again and sterilized the needle, thread, and other instruments, and brewed the Willow Bark tea Clawson had thoughtfully purchased. Albert laid everything on a tray with clean toweling over it and went into the bedroom.

Kirsty was still on the bed, although her face had a pale cast and a sheen of sweat. She'd kicked away the blanket he'd laid over her. He touched her arm lightly. "Kirsty," he whispered. "I'm going to bandage your knee and apply some medicine. It will sting. Can you hear me?"

She nodded and licked her lips. He would wait and give her water when he was done in case she became ill as he worked on her. He pulled the blanket and sheet away from her legs and began to pick away the small stones that were wedged in her knee under her skin. She moaned and bit her lip as he applied the ointment Clawson had provided.

Albert turned his attention to the cut on her thigh. The bleeding had stopped, but as he ran his finger over the jagged edge of her skin, she cried out. There was a piece of broken glass still in her leg; he could just feel the tip of it. There was no good in telling her to brace herself for pain. She undoubtedly would tense up and make it more difficult to extract the glass. He piled some toweling on either side of her leg, bent close to her, and caught hold of the glass with the pincher instrument Clawson had also thoughtfully provided. He held her leg still with one hand and slowly pulled out the piece of glass. It was longer than he'd anticipated, and the wound bled profusely. She arched off the bed, cried out, and then fainted. It was all Albert could do to continue. To cause her pain, discomfort, agony was nearly more than he could bear even knowing he did it so she could live. He threaded the needle and made eight tiny stitches to close the wound.

He folded toweling tight on her leg, the bleeding finally slowing and the stitches holding. He looked up to see her awake and staring at him.

# CHAPTER 14

"That hurt." She focused on his face, trying to lessen the pain in her leg that radiated to her toes. "What happened?"

"There was a piece of glass in your leg, most likely from when I p-pulled you through the window. I thought for certain that I'd cleared all the fragments from the frame, but I must have missed one. I'm so sorry for you to be in such p-pain."

"You saved my life," she whispered, feeling tears gather in her eyes. "How did you even know where I was?"

He told her then, embarrassed and regretful for his mother and cousin's plotting. "I do not think they understood the real d-danger they put you in. They were told some shelves would be knocked down and windows broken. I don't believe they had any idea that Cartwright had contacted this Plowman fellow."

"Cartwright?"

"That fellow you danced with at the Vermeal ball. Freddie was to meet him in the alley near your warehouse. Freddie would be d-dead too if I hadn't sent him with a message for your brother."

"Dead?"

"Cartwright was lying in the alley when I carried you away

once your brother arrived. I didn't stop to check him, but even at a glance I would say he was dead."

"I have caused all sorts of problems, have I not? I found something about Mr. Cartwright to be not quite trustworthy, but I never wished him dead. Yet I'm so tired I can't think it all through. I feel as though I could sleep for a week."

"You've lost a considerable amount of blood. You need rest."

She looked at him as he rolled down his sleeves and rubbed the back of his neck. He bent over and gathered things from the end of the bed. "You are exhausted too," she said. "Put those things away and come lie down."

"No. I couldn't," he said and went into another room carrying a tray.

He came back and sat on a chair at the edge of the room. "I will rest here while you sleep."

"I will stand up and walk—or crawl, if I have to—out of here if you do not climb into bed beside me," she said. "Please?"

The longing was clear on his face but . . . of course, he was a good man. An honorable one. How could she have thought about letting him get away from her? She would learn to deal with his mother whether they lived with her or not.

"Please, Albert. I want to feel your arms around me."

He stood and awkwardly shucked his shoes. She slowly shifted over in the bed while he fixed the linens under her legs.

"You must—" He stopped and cleared his throat. "You must m-marry me. And not because we are going to lay in a bed together."

He laid down and slid one long arm under her neck. She curled against him, her face on his shoulder. "Why must we marry," she whispered, "if it is not because we are in bed together?"

"Because I love you. I cannot l-live without you."

Tears welled in her eyes. "I love you so very much. I never thought I'd hear you say the same."

"I could not expect anything from you if I was not willing to give the same. My mother—dear Lord, my mother is a t-terrible person. I have ignored it because I was able to, but that was never going to be the case for a wife or for anyone in her power. I don't know anything about this family love you t-talk about, although I'm certain my father loved me. I'm willing to learn if you and your family are willing to teach me."

She nodded and touched her lips to his chest as she settled closer to him. Her eyes drifted shut. She was home.

ALBERT WOKE SLOWLY, STRETCHING HIS ARMS OVER HIS HEAD and wondering briefly where he was. He sat up, letting the blanket fall to his lap, and heard the singsong humming of his bride-to-be from the other room. He smiled; he couldn't help himself. He was in a lumpy bed, covered in scrapes and bruises, hungry and thirsty, still worried about dangerous men and his beloved's wounds, and yet he was happy and content with their small and not-quite-clean quarters. She was there with him, and that was really the only thing that mattered. He padded barefoot to the kitchen.

"What are you doing up so early?" he asked. "How do you feel?"

She turned and hurried to him, favoring her leg a bit. She threw her arms around his waist and looked up at him with a smile. "I wanted to wash myself and this dress before you got up, and I wanted to see if I could get a glimpse of your new house."

He tilted her chin up with his finger. "Our house," he said, thinking of her brother's advice to state his wishes in a confident way. "It will be our house as soon as I can c-convince you to marry me."

"I am already convinced."

"How is your leg? I should look at it," he said.

"It does not hurt much, surprisingly. I washed it and put some of the salve Mr. Clawson sent on it, so the stitches do not pull."

"That reminds me." Albert hurried to the window. "I told Mr. Clawson to bring food around this morning. Ah, there he is. Wait here and I will be back with our breakfast."

He hurried back quickly, his stomach growling, watching the street and alley for anyone suspicious. Kirsty took the bag from him when he came back and began pulling out its contents. Bread, hot and crusty, a jar of soup, apples, a wedge of cheese wrapped in a towel, slices of ham, and a pastry with filling leaking out of one end.

"Mrs. McClintok must have sent this. I would recognize her cherry turnovers anywhere." Kirsty smiled.

"I can't remember when I ate last," he said, staring at the food.

"Sit down, then," she said. "I've got the stove warm and will heat this soup. We will have soup and ham sandwiches."

Albert's stomach growled, and he blushed. Kirsty laughed.

"I'm going to have to make sure you're eating, I suppose. I think you forget sometimes."

"I do forget," he said as she put a bowl of steaming soup in front of him a few minutes later.

"Go ahead," she said. "Start your soup. I'll sit down when the sandwiches are made."

Albert jumped up from his seat. "I've forgotten my manners, sitting down while a lady is standing."

"We are on the run from bad men, Albert. It is fine that we are informal. Eat your soup. I can tell you're near starving."

He sat reluctantly, unable to resist the tempting smell of the soup. Kirsty placed a sandwich beside his bowl, and he made himself slow down. It would do him no good to eat so fast he made himself ill. He helped her with her chair when she put her dishes opposite him. There was something very intimate about their tableau. Something that spoke of family meals, and he had to calm himself as he thought of it—maybe even children. He glanced at her.

"What are you thinking, Albert? Your face is bright red."

He cleared his throat. "I was thinking, just wondering, if at some t-time in the future there would be children at our t-table."

She smiled and looked at him from beneath her lashes. "I certainly hope so."

His heart pounded in his chest. "I thought perhaps you would want t-to wait, with your business just beginning."

"Plenty of mothers in my neighborhood have children and work outside the home. Many of them have to, if they are widows or if they need the income, or maybe if they want to. The oldest child tends the youngest, or a grandparent or an aunt may. Muireall and Aunt Murdoch raised us. Families find a way."

"They do, don't they? We'll have an income that will allow us to choose what we wish to do if we are b-blessed with children."

She blushed and busied herself with her meal. When they were finished eating, he washed the dishes, something he'd never done in his entire life, letting them dry on the side of the sink. He wrapped the cheese and the pastry in cloth and set it aside. There was no ice in the icebox, so it was just as well they'd finished most of the food, but then he must begin thinking about what they would eat that evening.

"I'm going to lay down for a nap. I think all the emotions from yesterday have caught up with me." She gave him a suggestive look. "You're probably tired, too."

Suddenly, the air crackled between them, making him short of breath and wanting. She turned and went into the bedroom, the door still open as she pulled her dress over her head, leaving her in her chemise and lacy drawers. She glanced at him over her shoulder as she pulled a few pins from her hair and it tumbled over her shoulders. He followed her into the bedroom and pulled off his boots. She'd already climbed into bed, lifting the blankets for him to join her. He lay flat on his back, his breathing short, feeling as though he stood at the edge of a very steep cliff, preparing to step off into the unknown.

KIRSTY ROLLED ONTO HER SIDE AND PUT HER HEAD ON HIS shoulder. He was breathing rapidly, and she could feel his heart pounding against her ear. She gently touched the cut on his lip and one above his eye. She picked up his hand where it lay and kissed the cuts and the wrapped fingers.

She tilted her head up and kissed the underside of his chin, letting her hand roam across his chest, stopping halfway to run her fingers through the dark hair there.

"Kirsty, darling. This may l-lead us to do something we may r-regret."

"What could we regret?" she whispered in his ear, letting her breath, warm and moist, touch him. He groaned.

"That we d-did not wait to be properly wed to . . . to . . ."

"To make love, Albert?" she asked, and he groaned again. "I don't want to wait, not one more minute."

He gently closed his hand over hers, stilling her motions. "I c-cannot believe that you see me that way. As a . . . as a l-lover. I'm not the t-type of man who stirs beautiful women to their p-passions."

"You think I'm beautiful, Albert?"

He rolled onto his side to face her and held her chin. "You are kind and clever and giving, which is the most important thing a p-person can be. Your beauty comes from within." He examined her face from her forehead to her eyes to her chin. "But that is besides the fact that you are a perfectly beautiful woman who I dream about at night and, like Helen of Troy, could launch a thousand ships."

He ran his hand down her arm and to her waist, spreading his fingers in a possessive grip. She pulled his hand to her breast.

"I am in love with you, Albert. You are the most handsome,

brilliant man I've ever met and the only one I want to show me the mystery of physical love."

Albert rolled her onto her back, leaning over her, his hand kneading her breast, and kissed her passionately. His tongue circled her lips, and she opened to him. She held his face with both hands on his cheeks, her eyes drowsing with the heat of their kisses. He moved his tongue in and out of her mouth, and her hips surged against him. He moaned and turned onto his back, throwing back the blanket and standing to remove his pants and drawers.

She stared at him wide-eyed as that part of him, that part that was long and jutting out from him, surrounded by dark hair, was revealed. Just the sight of him made her pant with want, glancing up at him as his chest rose and fell too. She rid herself of her chemise and drawers, stretching out before him, watching him run his eyes over her naked body. She thrust out her breasts.

He climbed in beside her, running his hands over her, licking her nipples and slowly sucking until she felt as if she could not breathe. He stretched his hand over her stomach and between her legs, slipping a finger inside her. She gasped and pumped her hips against him.

"Kirsty, love," he said, panting with each word. "Lay on your back and let me between your legs."

She stretched out, spreading her legs wide, feeling no shame, only that this man, this perfect man, wanted her and all her passions. He moved his hips, bringing himself against her open womanhood, his arms held straight on either side of her.

"This may hurt, my darling. There is no way to—"

But she'd been impatient, even impetuous, all her life and was no less at this moment as the tip of him grazed her. She grasped his bottom, his perfect muscular behind, and pulled him inside her with one swift thrust. They both groaned, he breathing heavily above her, and she taking small breaths as she worked through the fierce pain that was, thankfully, short-lived. And then he moved in her.

"Oh my dear Lord," she said breathlessly. "That is, this is, oh, faster, Albert. Please."

He complied, entering and withdrawing, continuing slowly at first but then faster and with more intensity, making the room, the danger, the world spin away from her, leaving her senseless and satisfied and limp. He dropped down on one elbow, bent his back to bring his face to hers, and kissed her. "I love you," he whispered and pumped harder and faster until he stopped and gasped for breath, shaking and moaning.

He dropped onto her, quickly rolling onto his back and bringing her with him to hold tightly at his side.

DEAR GOD! ALBERT'S MIND WAS A WHIRL. HE MUST MARRY THIS woman and do it quickly. He sat up, feeling guilty, and pushed the covers away.

"Have I hurt your leg or, well, any other part of you? I've been unfeeling and may have torn your stitches for my own pleasure," he said hurriedly.

She shook her head and pointed to her leg. "The stitches are fine. Not even pulling. And as for other parts," she said, a grin on her face, "other parts will recover quickly, I think, Albert."

He could feel the heat of a blush rise from his chest to his face as he was already wondering when she would be feeling up to making love again. Dear Lord! What was the matter with him? He'd just taken the virginity of a gently bred young woman outside the vows of marriage. What kind of villain was he?

"Albert?" he heard from behind him.

"I'm to b-blame for all of this. I will make it right, I p-promise you. Whatever must be done or said to make this right will be d-done."

Kirsty crawled around him to the edge of the bed and stood

naked before him. She picked up a few pins from a side table where she'd laid them and pulled her glorious hair up in a loose knot, pinning it in place. She wrapped herself with a length of sheeting he'd brought in the room in case her leg began to bleed. She had no idea how gorgeous and provocative she was, barefoot, with tumbling hair, her shoulders bare, and her breasts just covered with the sheet. He cleared his throat.

"Are you saying you won't marry me, Albert?" she asked.

He looked at her, stricken. "What are you talking about? Of course I'm going to marry you. If you'll still have me."

"Then why have you become so morose?"

"I should have been able to control myself. I'm a man, not a boy. I p-pushed myself on you, and you couldn't have been ready as we are not even married! It is too much! This should have never happened. Here we are in carriage house, on a filthy bed, carrying on as if—"

"We are going to have our first argument," she interrupted. "We both agreed to lay together. We've committed ourselves to marriage. And you insist on ruining what was the most precious, exciting, meaningful moment of my life. I've found my love in you and have given myself to you to express my love for you. And you are making it cheap. I am angry right now in case you hadn't realized."

She was formidable in addition to being beautiful and spirited and courageous. She picked up her clothes from where they were scattered and hurried into the kitchen, holding her sheet together at her neck. He could hear chairs slamming against the table and quiet, angry murmurs. He was not quite sure what to do or what he'd done, but he certainly did not mean to face her stark naked and hurriedly put his clothes on. He was pulling on his boots when he heard the door slam.

Albert hopped through the kitchen to the stairs carrying one boot. "Kirsty! Dear Lord! Where are you going?"

He flopped down on the first step to pull on his second boot and heard the horse below nicker. By the time he was down the stairs, she was leading that horse to his carriage. She was still muttering.

"Stop! You must stop, Kirsty! It could be dangerous!"

"Plowman's men have no idea where I've gotten to, and I intend to go home to Locust Street while they are looking elsewhere. I want a decent meal and a bath. I want to think about how insulting you've been," she said as her voice cracked and her eyes filled with tears. "Either hitch the horse or get out of my way."

He was completely and utterly out of his depths. "I'll take you."

She continued hitching the horse to the cart and led him out of the stable into the alley behind the carriage house. She climbed in herself, refusing his hand, and settled on the seat. He jumped in beside her and picked up the reins.

# CHAPTER 15

Kirsty knew she was being unreasonable, but she truly needed to be home, although she suspected that the only home for her in the future was wherever Albert was. He slowed the horse as they neared Locust Street and then set off at a brisk pace until he was directly in front of number 75. She jumped down, hurried up the steps, and pounded on the door. She heard shouting from within and could feel Albert behind her.

The door opened, and she rushed into Muireall's arms.

"Kirsty! Thank God you are home!" Muireall whispered in her hair.

"Kirsty, girl? Is that you?" Aunt Murdoch hurried down the steps.

"It's me, Aunt. I just had to get home."

Muireall turned to Mrs. McClintok. "Tell Robbie to get messages to Elspeth and to James."

Aunt Murdoch hugged her and swayed back and forth. "I thought you were done for. My heart can't take it! You must never sneak out again."

"I'm done sneaking out." She glanced at Albert. "I need to bathe and change, and then I'll tell you everything."

. . .

SHE WASHED AND DISCARDED HER BLOODSTAINED CLOTHES, happy to pull on clean garments. She joined Albert, her aunt and sister, and feasted on all the foods Mrs. McClintok carried in on trays: tea, sandwiches, cheese, cake, and chocolate-covered toffee that the housekeeper knew was Kirsty's favorite. She'd worried them all, knowing that but realizing it fully when Payden ran upstairs from the kitchen where the family produced their canned goods, sweat pouring down his face, and grabbed her in a tight hug. He released her quickly, suddenly self-conscious, it seemed, but long enough to know he'd been very worried about her. Robbie McClintok stood behind him.

"I'm very glad you're home, Miss Thompson," he said.

"I'm glad to be home, Robbie," she said as she kissed his cheek and felt tears in her eyes.

"Now tell us," Muireall said softly. "Where have you been the last two days? James and Alexander have told us what happened at your shop. I've hired Mr. Caruso, the handyman we often use here, to secure your storefront."

"Oh, thank you, Muireall. I hate to know what those men ruined, but I am more concerned about Alexander. Please tell me. Is he well?"

Muireall nodded. "Yes. Elspeth is fussing over him every second, and he is enjoying the attention from what I can tell. The bullet just grazed his arm. It did not even need stitches."

"I was so worried," she said and looked at Albert standing behind the chairs they'd gathered in, his back to a bookcase. "Albert said not to worry because Alexander was fighting someone when he ran by."

"He was right. James said Mr. Watson acquitted himself well during the scuffle and that he scooped you up and ran straight through Plowman's men."

"I don't remember. There was a man holding me, and I bit his arm, but then he hit me. I don't know if the blow knocked me out or if it happened when I hit the ground. I remember nothing after biting him."

"James said you were fighting them by yourself when he and Alexander arrived, Mr. Watson," Muireall said. "We're all so grateful you were there to defend our Kirsty."

"I was in the basement hiding when I climbed on a desk to look out the window, and there he was fighting them off. And then he broke the window and pulled me through into the alley," she said and swallowed. "They would have found me in the cellar, and there was nowhere to run. I was trapped until Albert rescued me."

Muireall's eyebrows rose. "Thank goodness for *Mr. Watson*."

"There's no longer a need to be formal with him, Muireall." She stared steadily at her sister.

"Kirsty? Kirsty?"

"In here," Kirsty said and jumped from her chair. She and Elspeth met at the doorway in a long hug. Kirsty released her sister and hurried to her brother-in-law, who was holding a sleeping Jonathon. "Alexander, are you well? Truly well? I'm so very ashamed and so sorry to have put you in danger."

"I am fine, Kirsty. Dr. Gibson looked at my arm and declared it did not even need stitches."

"Kirsty, you cannot blame yourself! You did not fire that gun," Elspeth said in a trembling voice.

"Where is that *girl*?" they heard from the hallway.

Within moments, Kirsty was wrapped tight in James's arms. "Our prayers are answered." He held her away from him then and glanced at Albert. "Where have you been?"

"Come. Sit down, and I will tell you." She seated herself on the chair near the bookcase. Albert, stood next to her, his hand on the back of the chair near her shoulder in a proprietary manner.

"After he carried me away from the shop—oh, Muireall,

Albert says that Donald Cartwright was in the alley near my shop, and he was dead."

Muireall glanced at him. "I didn't know that. How was he mixed up in any of this?"

"Before Miss Thompson continues, I want you to know the p-part my mother and my cousin played in this."

"Your mother?" James said.

"She was unsatisfied with the outcome of her scolding of Kirsty at the Library Association luncheon, wasn't she, Mr. Watson?" Lucinda asked.

"I could not say. However, she has been upset with me for several r-reasons, but especially in regard to my pursuit of Miss Thompson to be my wife," he stopped to clear his throat. "Although I'm certain you are aware that your sister rejected my p-pursuit."

"And your cousin?"

"My cousin, my mother's brother's son, is our only other r-relative here in America. He is jealous, I believe, of me and the size of the estate that has been left to me by my father. He and my mother paid Cartwright several thousand dollars to v-vandalize Miss Thompson's storefront. I found out about it quite by accident when I went to speak to my m-mother about a separate residence I'd recently purchased for myself. They knew nothing about this fellow who is after your family. They only dealt with Mr. Cartwright, who I believe was the one who was involved with this Plowman fellow."

Kirsty glanced at Aunt Murdoch, who was smiling. "Ah. A new address for a bachelor."

"Yes. I am hoping Miss Thompson will be amenable to my suit if our future home is separate from my mother," he said and glanced at Kirsty.

"There are other things that must be settled before a final decision is made," she said.

. . .

## THE PROFESSOR'S LADY

THIS WOMAN MADE HIM FORGET HIMSELF. SHE MADE HIM anxious for her nearness and hungry for her body and desperate for the glimpses of what his life would be with her at his side. But right now she was being so contrary that he could hardly think straight, which made him forget there were others in the room.

"Kirsty, it is imperative that we m-marry and do so r-right away."

"Are you certain, Albert? You didn't seem certain today after . . . afterward. I won't be coerced."

"C-Coersion? There is no intimidation required. We must marry!"

Kirsty stood suddenly. "It's been a long few days, and the stitches in my leg are aching. I'm going to my room for a lie down."

"Stitches?" Muireall asked.

"When Albert pulled me through the window, I got a piece of glass in my leg right here." She pointed to her upper thigh. "He removed the glass and stitched it closed, but now the stitches are pulling and itchy. I'll be in my room."

Kirsty walked out, and Elspeth and Lucinda followed her. Albert watched her leave, an oath dying on his lips, and realized he was not alone.

"Muireall? Aunt Murdoch? Would you give us the room and take Payden with you?" James said.

"I'm old enough to hear what you are going to say to him!" Payden shouted. "She's my sister too, you know!"

"You're not old enough for this conversation, especially as it relates to our sister, and you are not married. Go with Muireall," James said.

The room emptied other than James, Alexander, and himself. He had no idea what they were going to say but he was not going to lie down and let them walk all over him with their superiority and . . . manliness. He was just as much a man as either of them, and he knew that he must control the conversation, or he would be in this very room for the next twenty or so years. The two men were staring at him.

"Kirsty and I made love. It's possible she could be expecting a child. I'm going to marry her and do it very soon."

Both men's eyes opened very wide.

"Albert!" Alexander said. "I have vouched for you with this family."

"You may vouch all you wish. This business is between Kirsty and myself. I love her. I've bought a property apart from my mother, who can be a harridan, for us to set up a household. I will do what I have to do to make the ceremony happen quickly, but there's never been a question of our honor. We committed to each other, and that bond is as unbreakable as any I will give in the future whether in a church or by law."

"Then what is the problem?" James asked.

"You have not stuttered once, Albert," Alexander said.

Albert could feel his face redden as he remembered the scene in the carriage house and how badly he'd bungled the conclusion of their lovemaking, especially as she'd been a virgin—of course she was a virgin—and needed to have her first man, and her last man, to be loving and caring and sentimental. She did not need his confusion and guilt. He dropped down into the chair behind him and ran his hands down his face.

"After . . ."

Alexander nodded. "Yes. After . . ."

"I was not, I did not, I mean, I . . . maybe cold. Upset."

"Surely you . . ." James said, and Albert shook his head.

"No, I . . ."

Alexander looked away. "Nothing tender, then, or . . ."

"I think she was expecting . . ."

"Good God, man, of course she was," James said. "Men need the physical. Women want the emotional. Didn't anyone ever tell you that?"

"Who would tell me that?" Albert asked angrily. "And that's

not true. I see how you look at your wife! You worship her! And you, Alexander, you were a blubbering, emotional mess when your wife gave birth. You would have cut off an arm to save her the pain."

James pointed at him. "But we are not the ones accused of being cold, are we?"

"You'd better make this up to her, Albert. Kirsty has a mind of her own, and she deserves some romance and some wooing. There were hordes of men who wanted to court her. She's never been more than pleasant with any of them until you came along."

"Alexander's right, you know. This calls for a grand gesture. Because if there's any chance she is expecting without a ring on her finger, it will not go well for you." James stared at him, leaving him in little doubt that he would make Albert's life miserable, or maybe end it, if he was unable to get her to a church. "Happy wives make for a pleasant household. Alexander and I can tell you that with certainty."

"Mr. Watson seemed very upset when you left the room," Elspeth said.

Kirsty untied her petticoat and pulled up her skirt and her drawers. She stepped in front of the long mirror in the corner of her room. "I wonder if I'll have a scar."

"But what about Mr. Watson?" Elspeth repeated.

She dropped her skirt. "I imagine he is upset. I was very angry with him, and I am still."

"What are you angry about?" Lucinda asked.

"I'm sure both of you understood from our conversation that we had relations, marital relations, while we were hiding from the Plowmans," she said.

"Oh, Kirsty. That is quite a serious step, especially if you are not quite sure you will marry him."

"I'll marry him," she said. "I love him, and he loves me. There is no one else for me, I'm certain of it, but that does not mean I am not angry."

"What did he do?" Lucinda asked. "Men can be so obtuse, and I'm thinking that a man as cerebral as Mr. Watson may be oblivious on some subjects."

"Oblivious is a good description. We made love," Kirsty said and turned to stare out the window of her room, reliving the passion, the way he looked at her, his love words. "It was glorious. All of it. I knew the mechanics but could never have dreamt the reality." She looked at the other two women. "And then he ruined it."

"Oh dear." Elspeth clasped Kirsty's hands in hers. "Surely he did not mean to ruin such a beautiful moment."

"I was so happy. So content. Imagining he was feeling the same astonishment about what we'd done. But he sat up, head in his hands, and began reciting how horrible a person he was and how we should have waited and how he would make it right. He cheapened what was perfect for me, and it made me very angry."

"That is because Mr. Watson is an honorable man. It's obvious that you love each other very much. You will work this out, I'm certain of it."

"Best to get on with the ceremony regardless."

"But I am still angry. I do not want to lay my hand in his at the altar while I am seething!"

Lucinda smiled. "You are underestimating your brother and brother-in-law. They are talking about this very thing right now, although there are most likely more grunts and half sentences with the men's conversation than the one we are having, but still, they will give him their experienced advice on marital matters."

"Yes." Elspeth smiled. "They will tell him to do whatever is necessary to make you happy."

Muireall opened the door of the bedroom. "Now that you are home and safe, I am going to the orphanage. I've told Mrs. McClintok we will eat at six." She looked at Kirsty. "We can begin making some wedding plans at that time. And Aunt has rocked Jonathon to sleep and laid him in the crib in your old room, Elspeth. When are you going to tell us you are in a family way, Lucinda?"

Lucinda smiled. "Right now, I suppose. I'll be presenting James with a son or daughter in the spring. I've just confirmed it with the doctor this week."

Kirsty hugged her. "How exciting! A cousin for little Jonathon!

# CHAPTER 16

"Mr. Graybell?" Albert said as he knocked on the butler's workroom on the lower floor of Charterhouse Square.

"Mr. Watson! How may I help you?" Graybell said and hurriedly wiped his hands. "You needn't venture down here. I would be glad to attend you above stairs."

Albert turned to the door. "Ah, Mrs. Munchin. Please join us." He waited until both were settled in their seats, now staring up at him in confusion.

"I hope there is nothing you've found that does not meet your satisfaction, Mr. Watson."

"Oh no. That is not it at all. I wanted to tell you that I've purchased a home for myself and for Miss Thompson, who hopefully will agree to marry me very soon. I will still oversee things here but will not be living here. You've both served our family well and you are welcome to stay on in your current position, or, if either of you would prefer, I can release the retirement that my father invested for you. I think you would both be able to live comfortably on the interest if you would like."

Both employees stared at him, Mrs. Munchin shifting in her seat, a worried look on her face. Graybell spoke first.

"I am not quite ready to retire and am perfectly comfortable continuing on here if my work is to your satisfaction."

"Of course it is, and you are welcome to stay," Albert said. "Mrs. Munchin?"

"Well, sir," she said hesitantly. "I would like to continue working, but . . ."

Graybell looked at the housekeeper. "What Mrs. Munchin is attempting to say, I would guess, is that her position here would not be secure, or perhaps not be as satisfying for your family when you are no longer living here. Am I correct, ma'am?"

"Yes, Mr. Graybell," she said and looked up at Albert. "I'm often not able to fulfill my duties to Mrs. Watson's satisfaction. And I believe she would be less satisfied if you are no longer living here."

How blind he'd been to his own mother's behavior. He was most ashamed of himself.

"I would have to consult with Miss Thompson, but perhaps you would like to be the housekeeper at my new home? It is significantly smaller and—" he stopped to clear his throat. "And there may be children in that household in the future, something you have not been forced to deal with here."

Mrs. Munchin's face lit up. "Oh, Mr. Watson. Please do ask Miss Thompson if she would consider me. I am not quite ready to retire and would be so happy serving a young family. My own daughter and her family live in New York, and I see them once or twice a year. I would surely love to be around children more often."

"Let me speak to her," he said, though he wouldn't be able to do so until she was speaking to him again. "What would we do here, Graybell, for a housekeeper? Is there someone ready to promote?"

"I think it might be wise for me alone to take Mrs. Watson's direction. Then I can direct the staff of her wishes. I'll promote someone to take on Mrs. Munchin's duties, but she will not have to attend Mrs. Watson personally for instructions. What do you think, sir?"

"I think the both of you have made this a well-managed and pleasant home in spite of obstacles beyond your control. Make whatever staffing changes you wish, Graybell. I'm off to announce these changes to my mother and my cousin," he said and stood. He smiled at them both. "Wish me luck."

ALBERT FOUND HIS MOTHER AND HIS COUSIN IN HER "DRAWING room." He was shocked that Frederick had returned to his home considering the last time he'd seen him and the threats he'd made, which he fully intended to keep. He strode into the room.

"Mother, Frederick," he said. He remained standing, hoping it lent him some command and knowing that these two people, two people who should have his best interests at heart, would always attempt to manipulate him, and he had no intention of changing his mind about anything he'd decided.

"When did you arrive, Albert? Graybell said nothing."

"He wouldn't have had a chance, Mother. I've been speaking to him in the butler's room for a few minutes."

"How many times have I told you to let the servants come to you? You set a poor example by attending them in their work areas."

"I will speak to them where I please, Mother."

She huffed. "There is no reason to be disrespectful, Albert. Your father would be ashamed of you."

"I agree he would be ashamed of me, but not for the reasons you think. In any case, I am glad I have found you both together as I wanted to let you know I have purchased a new home."

"What?" his mother said, her voice shrill. "Without consulting me? I don't want to move. I am comfortable here and getting on in years. I don't need the change in surroundings."

"That is just as well because you won't be moving. This new

home is for myself and my bride. You are welcome to visit, and I hope you will have a cordial relationship with her at some point."

His mother's expression was comical. He'd been worried that she would be hurt, but clearly that was not the case. She was furious. She jumped up from her chair.

"How dare you? How dare you? You will leave your mother alone in this cold house? No comforts from a son? You go too far!"

It pained him to see her so angry, but he knew he must hold his ground. "I've gone exactly as far as you have pushed me. Graybell is having my belongings packed as we speak, and Mr. Clawson will go with me." He turned to Frederick. "I will no longer be paying the lease on your townhome. You will vacate it or pay it yourself."

"Where am I to go?" Frederick asked.

"Do not give me that bewildered look you ply on Mother. You have until January to be gone when the lease expires."

"You will move in here with me, Frederick. I'll need a young man as my own son is abandoning me."

Albert was worried that she would make that offer, but he would tolerate it. He *did* hate to see her alone in this house, although it may come as a shock to her that Frederick did not spend all of his nights in his own home.

"You should take Mr. Clawson's rooms when you move in. Graybell can have them cleaned and painted, and there is plenty of furniture in other rooms that you can use to furnish them. There's a bedroom, a bathing room, a spacious sitting room, and a small office," he said. "And there is a private entrance."

Frederick went from wary to accommodating in a blink. He smiled. "Aunt Althea, I would never leave you alone here to fend for yourself. We will rub along just fine. And you never know. Perhaps someday Albert will need us." He turned to stare at him.

"One other thing I must make clear, Mother. You will never publicly disparage Miss Thompson or put her in danger ever again. You will be polite to her in public."

"I will do no such thing! She's not worthy of this family, and I will not stay silent when she surely embarrasses you."

"Let me be very clear, Mother. I will not tolerate an unkind word about her from you."

"Or what? What could you possibly do to hurt me any more than you have already done?"

Albert stared at her for a long minute, letting her know he was resolute. He did not want to threaten her. It wouldn't be right, and he couldn't bring himself to do it anyway, but she mustn't know that. She finally looked away from him, but she looked sad and very feeble, and it made him feel like the worst son who ever lived. But if he were to give her an inch at this moment, he would never marry the woman he loved desperately, or any woman for that matter. He would be wholly in his mother's power. He felt like he had come too far for that, made commitments with a new attitude and confidence. He'd learned that, as opposed to science and much of medicine, there was not always one answer to love, and to family.

KIRSTY WIPED THE PAINT FROM HER NOSE AND PUT THE BRUSH down after she finished touching up the trim around the front door. She turned in a circle, looking at the inside of her store. Mr. Caruso had fixed what Plowman's men had ruined and had the glazier's refit glass into one of the huge front windows. The glass painter would come the following week to gold leaf the windows to say *Thompson's Wools and Yarns*. MacAvoy, Alexander, and James had hung the door to the storeroom and set up the huge counter in the front. Muireall, Elspeth, and Lucinda had painted the walls, and Robbie and Payden had put a coat of varnish on the floors. Kirsty had come by every day with one Alexander's bodyguards to open the front and back doors and the transoms over the front entrance to let the cool autumn air blow through and take the last remnants of paint and varnish odors out of the building. Shelves and long tables had been installed in the back. The basement had been cleaned and aired and the window Albert had dragged her through had been repaired.

She was so excited she could barely contain herself. The only thing marring her mood was that she'd seen little of Albert. She'd gotten her courses and wanted to tell him there was no hurry for their marriage, but she hadn't seen him, and truthfully, she was ready to marry him anyway. She wasn't angry at him any longer, maybe a little disappointed, but wasn't all marriage about compromise? Most of all, she missed him.

He'd sent several letters, which she treasured, telling her he was finishing up two large projects. One at the hospital and the other getting his house ready for them to set up their home. It had needed a good cleaning and painting too. He and Mr. Clawson had lived in two of the rooms in the main house while the work was done there as well as on the lodging above the carriage house, including installing plumbing and a bathing room there. She had readily agreed to allow Mrs. Munchin to become their housekeeper and had met with her to discuss what would need to be purchased to outfit her new home.

Her new home! Her new husband-to-be! Her new business! Kirsty was so happy she could cry. The only thing missing was that bit of romance that she'd been hoping for, but Muireall had been practical and told her that she must be content that he was kind and had a good income and would always treat her with courtesy and respect. Her sister was right. Albert was a good man who loved her. How could she ever ask for more?

Once home, Kirsty spent a long hour soaking in the tub, washing her hair, and letting her sore muscles relax. Dr. Gibson had taken her stitches out and had finally declared her able to take a full bath rather than just a sponge bath in her room. She kissed her aunt and sister and brother good night and climbed the steps to her room. She pulled off her old battered robe and slipped into bed, closing her eyes the instant her head touched her pillow and waking with a start sometime in the middle of the night. Something was scratching at her window. She picked up a fireplace poker and peeked through the curtains.

ALBERT HAD NOT QUITE THOUGHT THROUGH THE PARTICULARS of carrying off his fiancé in the middle of the night. He had a fingerhold on the cement windowsill outside of her bedroom and a toehold on the mortar space between the bricks after climbing up a downspout. He was not made for this kind of intrigue and had an internal guffaw that he was quite the caveman, come to carry off his "woman." He dug a finger under the sash, guaranteed by Aunt Murdoch to be unlatched. The curtain opened suddenly, shocking him enough that he nearly fell to the flagstones below him.

"Albert," Kirsty whispered after opening the window. "Whatever are you doing?"

Albert pulled himself—rather inelegantly, he had to admit—over the sill and onto the floor of her bedroom. He sat up and straightened his jacket. "I've come to carry you away."

"What?" she asked with a giggle, but Albert could see she was intrigued.

"I have come to carry you away. We've not seen each other for more than two weeks. I miss you," he said and cleared his throat. "I want you."

She smiled. "Then you'll be carrying me to the bed, I suppose."

"No. I have plans for us this evening. I'd intended to carry you down the way I'd come up, but I'm worried I will drop you."

"What are your plans?" she asked as she fiddled with the end of her plaited hair.

"It's a surprise, but we've got to figure a way out of the house in order to commence with my plans."

She knelt down beside him. "Perhaps we could walk down the

back staircase and go out the kitchen door. You'll have to take your shoes off."

"It sounds as if you've done this before."

"I'll tell you about the last time I did it, when Elspeth came with me to go see James fight. What a night that was."

Albert unlaced his shoes. "You'd best put some clothes on. It's chilly out, and we've got a few minutes in the open carriage."

Minx that she was, she pulled her nightgown over her head and stood in front of him, completely naked, the moonlight shining through the window, highlighting her full breasts. He hadn't forgotten how perfectly made her body was, but to see it in the flesh as opposed to his mind's eye was enough to make his body jerk in reaction. She was his.

She pulled on underclothes, stockings, and a loose dress and found a piece of paper and a pencil on a small desk in the corner of the room. She wrote something on it and laid it on her empty pillow. "Follow me," she said, shoes in her hand.

Albert followed her down the thankfully carpeted hallway past several rooms to a small door. She opened it slowly and disappeared into the darkness. He inched his toe to the edge of the opening and took a deep breath. Why did he have a sudden premonition that his whole life, the entirety of it, would be following this woman into whatever unknown stood before her? Into the dark, into the light, and sometimes into a previously unknown bliss.

He crept down the steps in total darkness, dragging his hand down the wall as he went, until he felt her hand on his chest to stop him. A sliver of dull light showed when she cracked open the door in front of her. She peeked around the corner and opened the door wider into the kitchen.

"What smells so good?" he whispered.

"The dough for Mrs. McClintok's breakfast rolls is rising in that crockery bowl with the towel over it. Did you forget to eat, Albert?"

"Can we hire a cook that makes food like she does?"

Kirsty smiled and pulled a key from her skirts. "Yes, of course. Quiet now, while I open this lock."

His carriage was in the alley as he'd left it, except now the man who worked for Alexander Pendergast's security was stroking his horse's head. The one who'd been guarding Kirsty the afternoon he'd kissed her in the carriage.

"Hello, Mr. Bamblebit," Kirsty said. "Lovely evening for a ride, is it not?"

"Is it, Miss Thompson?"

"Oh, it is. You've met my fiancé, have you not?"

"I've observed him, yes," Bamblebit said with a nod and a scowl.

Albert nodded back and hurried to Kirsty's side to hand her into his carriage and climb in beside her. Soon they were passing her sister Elspeth's home and rolling down the alleyway to his carriage house. He took her by the hand and led her to the back door of the main house. It was completely dark until he lit a candle on a small table near the door.

"The house is not finished yet, well, most of it is not finished," Albert said and led her by the hand up a wide staircase that looked to be at the side of the main entrance. "Some of it is done. But much of it will have to wait until you have time to choose colors and furniture and whatnot."

"Oh, Albert," she said. "I've dreamed of decorating my own house. Are you certain we will have enough income for this home? It seems so large, although I've barely seen it."

"We will be fine. I'm having gas lights installed everywhere and bathing chambers too, although the work is not finished in much of the house. The only thing that is complete are these rooms," he said as he slowed his steps in the hallway. He opened a door and motioned for her to proceed him inside.

Kirsty walked in a few steps and stopped. There was a cheery fire burning in a fireplace opposite a huge bed with a beautifully carved headboard and footboard with matching tables on either side. The walls were papered in an extravagant yellow flower design, and the room was decorated with dark green curtains and spreads and pillows. She turned to him.

"This is so beautiful. It is exactly what I've always dreamed of having," she said, her vision blurry with tears.

"Mrs. Pendergast was very helpful. It seemed as though the two of you had discussed this sort of thing over the years."

"Oh yes. Elspeth and I spent many an afternoon planning and dreaming about when we'd marry and what our homes would be like. This is perfect."

"Let me show you your sitting room and office." He led her through a door she'd not noticed before.

"My office?"

"Every businesswoman should have an office," he said. "If you'd prefer it to be on the main floor, everything can be moved."

The sitting room had a marble fireplace, and the furniture was all warm blue and rose and gray. She ran her hand over the back of the large settee opposite a comfortable-looking, overstuffed chair with a footstool.

"Albert," she whispered.

"Come," he said before she could get overly sentimental, and she let him lead her into the bathing chamber. Candles were lit all around a large marble tub filled to near the top, a bottle of champagne chilling on a table nearby.

She looked at him in wonder and watched his Adam's apple bob.

"I was such a fool that day in the carriage house. I didn't regret any of it, but I did act as if I did. I want to make it up to you."

She leaned down and ran her hand through the water. It was toasty warm.

"Mr. Clawson got much of it ready for me and has gone to stay with his mother tonight. We are alone here."

She walked to him and began to unbutton her dress. She sat and removed her shoes and hastily donned stockings. She pulled the ribbon from the end of her hair and shook it free of its braid. "Is that my bed in the other room? Or is that your bed in the other room?"

"It is—" Albert stopped and cleared his throat. "It is our b-bed. Our bed for the rest of our days together."

"Through thick and through thin," she said and pulled her chemise over her head.

Albert was staring at her like she'd seen her brother and brother-in-law look at their wives, like she'd always dreamed of having a man look at her.

"I'm so sorry, Kirsty, love. So sorry to have marred that special day."

She smiled up at him. "You are well on your way to making me forget it ever happened."

Kirsty reached up to wrap her hands around Albert's neck. She was completely naked, and he was still fully dressed, and there was something very compelling about leaning against him and feeling his jacket and vest rub the tips of her breasts. Her fingers worked through the short hair at the back of his neck and pulled his face down to hers, stopping his lips just shy of hers. He was breathing heavily, glancing at her lips and then farther down to her breasts and back to her face, as if his intent was to ravish her, which she hoped was part of his plan. She knew he'd wanted her when he'd kissed her and when they'd made love, but this need was different, intense and focused and a bit feral.

She latched her lips to his and ran her tongue over his teeth. He growled and pulled her flush to him. He ran his kisses into her hair and whispered.

"I thought we'd take our time in the bath, but I don't think I can wait."

Kirsty ran her hand up the front of his trousers, feeling his hard length against her palm. "Then take me," she whispered.

He snatched her up in his arms, never taking his eyes from her face, turning sideways to hurry through the door, to *their* bed. She ran her fingers up and down his neck where she held on to him. He laid her down, and she stretched out, propped up on her elbows, her breasts thrust up, one leg bent at the knee. He surveyed her from her face to her feet and began to tear at his clothes. She licked her lips.

"Kirsty, love," he said when he stretched out beside her, his hand on her stomach, his voice shaking. "You make me crazed. I'm used to a thoughtful process in all I do, but when I'm with you, I cannot think straight. I'm no longer Albert Watson. You make me . . ."

Kirsty ran her hand up his chest, through the smattering of hair, and down his arm, defined with muscle, until she reached his fingers. She picked up his hand and placed it on her breast. She sighed, and he growled. "I very much like *this* Mr. Watson," she said and grinned.

He rolled over her, his long hairy legs tangling with hers and his hard member rubbing her in the very spot that was aching for him. "Albert. Please," she whispered. "Please."

He entered her a bit at a time until he was embedded as far as he could go. Then he rolled onto his back, bringing her atop him.

"Oh," she said and then smiled slowly. "Oh."

Albert laid his big hands on her thighs as she began to move on him, finding her pleasure and bringing him to his brink.

"We've . . . got . . . to . . . marry . . . very soon," he said as he held her still and pumped into her, gritting his teeth and tilting his head back as he found his release.

Kirsty flopped down on top of him, her breasts pressed against his chest, kissing his exposed throat as their breathing slowed. He ran his hands up and down her back, slowly and with tenderness.

"I love you, Albert. So very much."

He held her cheeks and tipped her face to his. "I am the luckiest man in the world that you are here with me. I will honor you as long as I live and thank the Lord that you have blessed me with your love because I love you with everything I am. Will you marry me?"

"Yes, Albert. Yes. I will marry you."

# EPILOGUE

Mid-December

"Dear Lord, Kirsty," Albert said as he handed his coat to Mrs. Munchin. "That tree must be twenty feet tall!"

"It nearly is," she said and hurried to him, unwrapping the wool scarf from around his neck. "I told Mr. West I wanted a tree that was at least fifteen feet tall, and he found this one! Isn't it beautiful?"

"It smells good. I don't think I ever had a Christmas tree growing up. Mother always said they made too much of a mess and that they were for the 'lower orders.'"

"It is very sad that you never had a tree," Kirsty said. "Although I can hardly understand your mother complaining about the dirt. It's not as though she ever cleaned anything up, did she?"

Albert shook his head. "Of course not."

She wrapped her arms around his waist. "You can help me decorate the top. Quite an advantage, having a tall husband. I closed the shop early, and Mrs. Munchin and I went to Wanamaker's for decorations and ribbons."

"How is she settling in?"

"Mrs. Munchin? Wonderfully. I think it is hard for her to understand that I work in my shop rather than manage your household, but she is growing accustomed to it. She is a dear and a very hard worker."

"I think my mother was rather cruel to her," Albert said.

"Speaking of your mother, I have invited her for dinner and to help decorate the tree."

Albert kissed her forehead. "You invite her once a week, and she has yet to come. Did she even reply this time?"

"Not yet."

"Why do you put yourself through this?"

She looked up at him, wide-eyed. "She is your mother, Albert. Family is all we have, even if she can be rather unpleasant. She has been unkind to me several times but in the end we are married, living in our own home, and we must try and heal the hurts with your family. We must be the best people we can be even if she can not."

He pulled her close. "I'm still furious with her."

"I've also sent invitations to Caleb and Gladys and Mr. Clawson too. If she does come, it's good to have others in the room. Less chance she'll call me a hussy."

Albert laughed. "You are persistent."

"Elspeth is going to ask her to join us at the tearoom downtown one day soon. She is convinced she'll come when she finds out that Lucinda will be there. And maybe it will put to rest any speculation that we have continued our quarrel."

"Are your sisters still upset that we married privately? Without them?"

"The grand wedding plans were not very far along when we were married. Our wedding was perfect. You and me and the minister and his wife. There really isn't anyone else necessary, is there?"

"Elspeth cried when you told her we'd already married, if you remember."

"She did, but she loved holding a dinner for us afterward. And it was lovely. Of course, Elspeth is the perfect hostess, and with Lucinda and Muireall helping and all deciding on the menu and decorations and even the guest list, I think they were more than satisfied."

"I dreaded having so many in attendance, but it was really very nice." He kissed her forehead. "I do love you."

"I know you do. I love you too. Why don't you change clothes? Guests could be arriving anytime and the new cook has roasted a turkey and made several apple pies."

Albert hurried to the stairs, his long gait crossing the wide marble foyer quickly, taking three stairs at once on his way to their bedroom. "I'll be ready in a thrice!"

"Hello, Gladys! Caleb. So very glad you were able to come!" Kirsty said later that evening. "Oh, and here is Mr. Clawson too. Come in, come in!"

"Thank you for the invitation," Caleb Brock replied as Gladys Clark leaned forward to kiss her cheek.

"Our monthly luncheon was less merry without you," Gladys said. "But we'll have to excuse you as you were busy being married."

"I fully plan on attending in January." Kirsty led Gladys and Caleb to the sitting room as Mr. Clawson handed his coat to Mrs. Munchin.

"Hello everyone!" Albert said as he came through the door with Mr. Clawson.

Kirsty watched Albert pour wine for all, smiling and nodding, conversing with their guests and making everyone relax, even Mr. Clawson, who tended to be very quiet, especially with strangers.

She loved him. He was the perfect husband for her. He was convinced she made their home hospitable with comfortable furniture and beautiful drapes and art on the wall. She was certain his kindness and gentlemanly behavior was the real reason their home made every girlish wish she'd ever entertained come true.

She turned as the door to the room was opened by a white-faced Mrs. Munchin. Kirsty jumped up, thinking something terrible had happened, when she saw her mother-in-law follow the housekeeper into the room. She took a deep breath and went directly to her, hands outstretched.

"Lady Watson, I'm so glad you could join us. And Cousin Frederick! How happy this makes me!"

"Mother," Albert said, coming to the door to greet her. "We were hoping you could join us. And Frederick too."

Albert hoped his other guests could not discern that he was not happy to see either his mother or his cousin. He hoped his smile covered the animosity he still felt toward his own relations' abysmal treatment of the woman he loved with all of his heart. He was sure that Kirsty was happy they'd come, though, truly happy, optimistic enough to believe she could bring them around to be part of their family. He wasn't convinced she, or anyone, could do it, and he was not convinced he wanted her to, but he would be as cordial as his mother's behavior allowed.

"May I show you to the dining room, Lady Watson?" Kirsty asked.

His mother glanced at him, hoping, he imagined, to be escorted by her son. He followed along behind, leading everyone to their places at the table. The dining room was all soft blue colors and papered walls with brass sconces now lit, matching the tall candles flanking a winter arrangement of gourds, pine cones, and dried flowers on the table. Kirsty seated his mother beside her from where she sat at the foot of the table with Caleb on her other side.

After asparagus soup, Mrs. Munchin's nephew, a young man of fourteen who Kirsty had recently hired, carried in the turkey on a platter to oohs and aahs from everyone except his mother. Even Frederick's eyes lit up.

"Would you like to carve, Mr. Watson?" Mrs. Munchin asked.

"I would surely make a hash of it, Mrs. Munchin. Would you mind carving in the kitchens?"

"Not at all, sir. Come along, Ben."

"No fish course, young lady?" his mother said to Kirsty. "You have much to learn about managing a proper household."

Kirsty smiled. "Albert and I don't care all that much for fish, and he seems quite happy with all the meals Mrs. Munchin and I plan, don't you, dear?"

"Very happy. The meals are very similar to the ones I've eaten with your family on Locust Street. All delicious," Albert said as Mrs. Munchin rolled a cart into the room. She and Ben started each dish with he or Kirsty, and they passed the bowls and platters on to their guests.

"I'm to dish my own? You need a proper butler, Albert!"

"Oh no, Lady Watson. Let me serve you," Kirsty said and did just that with every dish. She was smiling as she did it, still conversing with Caleb or Gladys and even Frederick.

His mother was staring at his wife, and he had a dreadful feeling there was about to be an outburst that would ruin this lovely meal and all his beautiful wife's plans. Just as his red-faced mother opened her mouth, Kirsty leaned forward.

"Allow me to spread your napkin on your lap. Would you like me to cut your meat?"

"I am not an invalid, girl!"

"Excellent! Enjoy, then," she said and turned to Caleb. "So tell me about this new research you are working on with Albert."

And that, it seemed, stunned his mother into silence. Albert watched out of the corner of his eye as she eventually picked up her fork and ate. Frederick was eating heartily and flirting with Gladys. This was a small miracle in his estimation, a glimpse into how they would negotiate this merging of families. His wife glanced at him and winked.

. . .

Albert sipped on the whiskey Alexander had handed him as they stood in the sitting room at 75 Locust Street. His stomach growled. Loudly.

"My stomach has begun to eat itself," Alexander said in response. "It is no longer talking to anyone."

Albert smiled and turned to James, who had just joined them.

"Where in the hell is she? Should I start to worry?" James asked. They were waiting on Muireall, who had gone to the Sisters of Charity Orphanage, as she often did. "Did she say anything to you, Aunt Murdoch?"

Their aunt jumped in her seat. "No need to shout, boy. I was dozing."

Elspeth laid a hand on the old woman's shoulder. "Did Muireall say when she'd be home?"

"There's never a set time, and she did say she might be late today. That fellow that follows her around would have said if she was in trouble, surely."

"One of Alexander's security men was with her. It's usually Bamblebit, who I think is sweet on Mrs. McClintok," Elspeth whispered.

"Let's eat," Payden said. "I can hardly wait any longer."

"He's right," Lucinda said. "Muireall doesn't expect us to wait on her, I'm sure."

"That orphanage is lucky to have her, I say," James added.

"With all her ducks but one grown and married, she's got to look after someone," Aunt Murdoch said and turned to Payden. "Help me out of this chair and let's eat. James, you'll need to say the blessing."

Albert filed into the dining room and helped Aunt Murdoch and his wife into their seats. Mrs. McClintok came through the swinging kitchen door at the same time, and Albert was treated to the delicious aromas he'd been dreaming of. He and Payden eyed each other and the baskets on the table filled with hot rolls and covered with linen napkins.

"I'll beat you to the first one, Watson. You're a slow old man," Payden said.

Albert's lip twitched. "I have surgeon skills you've yet to develop, young whippersnapper."

"There will be no grabbing for one of those delicious warm-from-the-oven buns. I'm the eldest at this table and will choose one first!" Aunt Murdoch said with a smirk to a smatter of laughter.

"Do I hear Jonathon, Elspeth?" Lucinda asked.

"Just a whimper, I think. No, Alexander. You are not going to go pick him up every time he moves during his nap. I want him to sleep a bit since MacAvoy, Eleanor, and Mary are coming to the house for cards and some games later. You're all welcome to join us," Elspeth said and looked up and down the table.

"Haven't seen MacAvoy and his missus for two weeks." James looked at his wife. "I'd like to if Lucinda is up to it."

Albert had the strangest feelings, his throat tightening, his eyes blinking, as if he might cry in front of his wife and her family. *His* family now, he thought, bringing him closer to this embarrassing emotional brink. He could tease and laugh and be angry, and he would always be safe here and accepted. They would commiserate about losses and rejoice with him in victories, something that seemed very foreign to him. He desperately wanted his own home to be the same, and he knew Kirsty would make it so.

He thanked Mrs. McClintok for his stew as she handed it to him and eyed Payden as Aunt Murdoch took her time choosing her roll from the basket.

"Oh, there is Miss Thompson," Mrs. McClintok said. "I heard the front door close. Robbie, see if she needs help with her coat."

A few minutes later, all heads turned as Muireall walked into the dining room holding the hand of a young girl.

"Oh, I'm so glad you began eating," she said. "Everyone, this is Ann Marcus. She'll be joining us for dinner. Mrs. McClintok? Can we squeeze one more place here between me and Mr. Thompson?"

"Of course. I'll get the setting right away."

James moved his chair over to accommodate the other one Robbie carried into the room, the taller one from the kitchen used for children. Ann Marcus was a dainty child with dark hair in two long plaits and large brown eyes. Muireall helped her be seated as stew was placed in front of them both. The table was quiet, everyone concentrating on their meal, until Elspeth spoke up.

"What a lovely name Ann is," she said and smiled.

"My Papa named me," the little girl chirped.

"Papas always know best, don't they?"

The girl nodded and unfolded her napkin, laying it carefully across her lap.

"The stew is hot, Ann. Blow on it to cool it down," Muireall said and blew a breath over the spoonful she was holding. Ann mimicked her and took a bite.

"Oh, that is delicious, Miss Thompson."

"Not too fast, dear. Would you like a roll?"

"Yes, please. May I butter it?"

"Of course. My brother Mr. Thompson will help you."

James broke open a roll and put plenty of butter on each half. "Here you are, Ann. Just like I like them. Steaming hot with plenty of butter."

"Thank you, Mr. Thompson. We don't always have butter with our meals, but I do like it."

Mrs. McClintok came through the kitchen door carrying a glass and went to Ann's place. "Here you are, miss. A nice cold glass of milk."

The child's eyes widened, she picked up the glass with both hands, and took a large drink. She wiped her mouth with her napkin and smiled sunnily. "Thank you, ma'am."

"Ah, there is the doorbell. Robbie, can you see who is here?"

"Everyone is here. I wonder who that could be," Elspeth said.

"Ann! Ann! Are you here?" a man said as he came down the hallway. "Ann!" he bellowed.

"Papa! I am here, Papa!" Ann said as she wiggled out of her chair. She flew into the man's arms as he came through the dining room doorway.

"My girl! The nuns said you'd gone with someone, and I didn't know who that person was. You must never do that again," he said, holding her tight and kissing her face and hair.

Muireall rose. "The Sisters of Charity would have never allowed a child to be taken by a stranger, sir. They've known me for years."

He put his daughter down beside him and turned to her. "But I don't know you, and my Ann is most precious. I can't countenance her wandering off with strangers."

"Strangers? I have just explained to you that I am well-known at the orphanage. Ann had not eaten all day, thinking you were to return for her and that you would eat together. Should I have let this dear child starve because you were late returning? I think not," Muireall said, her voice rising.

The man looked away, turning his hat in his hand. "I was to be back from this appointment by midafternoon, but the man I was to speak to did not return until an hour ago."

"What appointment could possibly be so important that you would worry a hungry child?" Muireall replied, her face reddening with anger.

The man stepped close to her. "I was interviewing for a job, ma'am. A job I need to make sure Ann has food on the table and clothes on her back," he said loudly.

"Papa! The stew is delicious, and there is butter for the rolls! You may have mine, for I'm certain you have not eaten."

James stood, glancing from his sister to the stranger, smiled, and put out his hand. "James Thompson. Won't you join us for a meal?"

"Captain Anthony Marcus of the 42nd. Oh, no longer captain. Just Anthony Marcus now. It's a pleasure to meet you, sir."

"It's a pleasure to meet you too. And by the way, that's my sister you're arguing with—my unmarried sister, *Miss* Muireall Thompson. Let me get you a chair beside her."

# AFTERWORD

I hope you have enjoyed Kirsty and Albert's story, the third in the new *Thompsons of Locust Street* series. Muireall's story, *The Captain's Woman*, releases in 2023. The first book in the *Thompsons of Locust Street* series is *The Bachelor's Bride*, followed by *The Bareknuckle Groom*.

Other American set historical romance series:

*The Crawford Family Series* includes *Train Station Bride, Contract to Wed*, companion novella, *The Maid's Quarters*, and *Her Safe Harbor* and tell the tales of three Boston sisters, heiresses to the family banking fortune.

*The Gentry's of Paradise* chronicle the lives of Virginia horse breeders and begins with Beauregard and Eleanor Gentry's story, set in 1842, in the prequel novella, *Into the Evermore*. The full-length novels are set in the 1870's of the next generation of Gentrys and include *For the Brave, For This Moment,* and *For Her Honor*.

Reader favorites *Romancing Olive* and *Reconstructing Jackson* are American set Prairie Romances and *Cross the Ocean i*s set in both England and America.

## AFTERWORD

*Politics & Bedfellows* and *All the News* are my general fiction titles published under Hollis Bush.

Please leave a review where you purchased *The Professor's Lady* or on GoodReads or other social sites for readers. Thank you so much for your purchase. I love to hear from readers! Please follow me on FaceBook, Twitter, or on my website hollybushbooks.com, for book announcements. The first few pages of *Into the Evermore* and *The Bachelor's Bride* follows.

All the best,
Holly

# EXCERPT FROM THE BACHELOR'S BRIDE

Philadelphia 1868

### Chapter One

"No! No, you will not, James."

"I will do as I wish," he thundered, slamming his hand on the thick wooden table, making the crockery dance.

"I am the head of this family, and I say you will not breathe a word of this to our brother or sisters," Muireall Thompson said through gritted teeth.

"Head of the family, are you, lass?"

"I am the oldest."

"And a *real* sibling to boot," James said and marched out of the kitchen.

Elspeth hunched under the stairwell outside the kitchens and watched her brother hurry past, his leather boots slapping against the stone floors, nearly masking his whispered curse words. He slammed the door at the top of the steps. She jumped when Aunt Murdoch spoke to her, just inches from her ear.

"What are you doing, child?" she asked.

"I was eavesdropping on an argument between Muireall and James."

"Does anything good ever come from eavesdropping?"

"Nay. Never," Elspeth said. "But that won't stop me from doing it."

One side of Aunt's mouth turned up. "There's no denying you're a MacTavish, with that sassy tongue of yours."

"MacTavish, Aunt? I've heard you call one of us that on occasion, but I never understood why. Are they our ancestors? A clan we'd best forget?"

"Shush," Aunt Murdoch hissed. "Have you finished the mending? Or are you just lazing about, listening to others' private talks?"

Elspeth looked into Aunt Murdoch's filmy blue eyes. There were some mysteries surrounding her family, the Thompsons. Some secrets. She'd overheard snippets over the years as some had not realized she was in the same room with them, but lips immediately clenched when they did realize, or when her younger sister, Kirsty, or her younger brother, Payden, were nearby. Aunt knew all the secrets, she was certain, but she was just as certain that she would never reveal any of them.

"I need more blue thread to fix one of Kirsty's church dresses. I'll be going to Mrs. Fendale's for more."

"Then get there and get back," Aunt said and went through the door to the kitchens, no doubt to harass Muireall.

Elspeth found James in the parlor, repairing the floor where a nail had come up through one of the varnished boards.

"If you pound that any harder, you're going to fall through," she said, wondering what he could have possibly meant by *real sibling* when he was arguing with Muireall.

"Better than fighting with our sister," he said, each word punctuated by a pound of the hammer. He sat back on his heels and looked up at her as she pulled on her short linen jacket. "Where are you off to?"

"Mrs. Fendale's for thread."

"You shouldn't be going to that part of town alone," James said as he stood. "I have to see about this beet delivery today, but I'll take you tomorrow."

"I'll be fine, James," she said to his sputtering. She stopped at the front door and pulled on her bonnet, examining herself in the mirror above the marble table. James was still telling her she wasn't allowed to leave without him, as she was a stubborn and foolish girl, when she pulled the door closed behind her.

She set out north toward the edge of Society Hill where they lived, crossing Chestnut Street, enjoying the spring air. Streets were crowded with carriages and wagons and horses, and all types of people too. Elspeth's family knew their neighbors, and she waved at old Mrs. Cartwright sweeping her steps and watched Mr. Abrams shaking his finger at his children as their heads nodded in agreement. The sun was shining, one of the first March days to be warm, and it seemed as though everyone was out of their homes and enjoying the weather after a particularly long and cold winter.

Three blocks more and she was less likely to wave or shout a hallo. She stared straight ahead, glimpsing the swinging sign over the door of her destination, and did not listen to the ridiculous and inappropriate comments some young men were directing at her. In just their shirtsleeves, no jacket or four-in-hand tie, and even some without a vest, they were hanging about a stairwell to a basement or coal chute or leaning against the gas streetlight posts, hooting and hollering at each other and at others on the street. Once she crossed Arch Street into Southwark, the houses were a little shabby, the streets had a little more garbage strewn about, and the residents looked a little more downtrodden, but she could see Mrs. Fendale's Millinery shop, not half a block away.

Unfortunately, she'd have to pass the bawdy house—not that she was supposed to know it was a bawdy house or even know what a bawdy house was, but she did have ears and a brain between them and would have been hard-pressed not to understand the conversation she'd overheard between James and his friend MacAvoy. But as it was just ten in the morning, hopefully those ladies would still be abed. It was quiet as she passed by, with one lone woman hanging out a second-floor window in a sheer chemise, one shoulder strap hanging down her arm, with a shiny corset over top of it, which was scandalous enough, but it was red—bright, blood red! All satin and lace and nothing like her own white cotton undergarments. She wondered why a woman would want to wear such a thing, but then, with a second glance at the woman, now smiling at her and tapping a thin cigar against the brick sill, she knew. It would entice a man, but what kind? Surely not a good one! Elspeth shivered and hurried her steps.

A bell rang over her head as she entered the seamstress's shop. "Hello, Mrs. Fendale! How are you this beautiful spring day?"

"Miss Thompson! How good to see you after this long winter! What may I help you with? A new hat, perhaps?"

Elspeth shook her head. "Oh no. I'm just doing some mending and have run out of blue thread." She ran her fingertips over lace lying out on the glass-top counter. "How beautiful! Maybe I will take a yard or two of this to add to Kirsty's best dress."

"It's a very lovely lace, made right here in our neighborhood," Mrs. Fendale said with a smile. "How much shall I cut for you?"

"I think two yards. It will be perfect to liven up one of last year's dresses."

While Mrs. Fendale tied the cut ends of the lace and wrapped the purchases, her son Ezra came out from between the dark hanging curtains that led to the back of the shop where the seamstresses and hatmakers worked. His head dipped into a nod as he smiled shyly, and a blush crept up his face.

"Good morning, Ezra." Elspeth smiled at the younger man.

"G-G-Good morning, Miss Thompson," he said and swallowed.

"Here, Ezra." Mrs. Fendale handed her packages to him.

"Carry Miss Thompson's things for her until she crosses the street."

"I'll be fine, Mrs. Fendale. No need to take Ezra away from whatever work he's doing for you."

"His work will still be here when he returns, and I'll feel better knowing he's with you until you've passed this block," she said and shook her head. "To think that those hussies ply . . ." Mrs. Fenway glanced at her wide-eyed son and then at Elspeth and closed her mouth.

"Good day to you, Mrs. Fenway, and thank you," Elspeth said with a smile.

"Good day, Miss Thompson."

Ezra followed her out of his mother's shop, holding the wrapped lace under his arm. "You needn't walk behind me, Ezra." She took the lace from his hands and put it in her bag along with the thread.

The young man hurried to walk beside her, keeping pace with her swift stride. Elspeth tilted her face to the sun, feeling its warmth, letting it seep into her muscles and make her feel as if all things she'd dreamed of were possible. That pleasurable feeling did not last long.

"Get your hands off me, you filthy copper," a woman shouted.

Elspeth looked up at the doorway of the bawdy house she was nearing. There was an older man, with mutton chops and a nearly bald head, being dragged out the door by a younger man in a dark suit. The woman who had shouted, the one in the chemise and red corset Elspeth had seen earlier, was hanging on to the bald man's sleeve, trying to drag him back inside the brick row house. There were no policemen in sight, but a crowd had gathered, mostly consisting of the young men who'd taunted Elspeth on her walk to Mrs. Fenway's.

"'E ain't going nowheres until 'e 'ands over me fee," she screamed and yanked on the bald man's jacket. Elspeth heard a ripping sound. The woman reached around the bald man and kicked at the younger man with a pointy-toed shoe.

"Ouch," he said and rubbed his thigh with his loose hand. "Let go of him, and I'll pay you."

The woman spit at the younger man, and the bald one found his footing and cuffed the woman hard across the face. She crumbled to the stoop with a cry, holding her face in her hands.

"Fucking whore telling me what to pay," the red-faced bald man shouted to cheers from the crowd of popinjays.

The woman looked up from where she cowered, and Elspeth could see blood running from her nose and lip. She'd seen enough.

"Stop!" she shouted as she picked up her skirts and hurried up the steps. "Stop this instant!"

Elspeth crouched down and pulled a handkerchief from her drawstring bag. She handed it to the woman, who looked up at her guardedly. Elspeth leaned forward and dabbed the blood from the woman's chin and mouth while the young men on the street in front of the house continued their taunts. She stood quickly and turned to the bald man.

"Pay her! Pay her this minute," she said.

The young man stepped between them. "There's no reason for you to get involved, miss. Please be on your way."

She batted his hand away when he reached for her. "Don't you dare touch me! You and your . . . your father are here together? How disgusting you are!"

The crowd roared their approval, and she could see Mrs. Fenway and Ezra at the edge of the crowd. The shop owner said something to her son, and he raced down the street, away from his mother's shop.

"This is not my . . ." the young man said, clearly affronted.

"Then why are you here with him? What need do you have to frequent this house?"

The young man's mouth twitched, and that was when she noticed he was startlingly handsome. Strikingly so. The crowd on the street was taunting him, asking him to tell her about his need. She felt her face go red and wished she could have taken back her words, but it was too late. She would have to brazen it out and was about to repeat her question when the bald man leaned close to her.

"What do you know of this house, girl? Are you looking to audition? I'll be happy to recommend you if you meet my expectations." He let his eyes drift down to her bosom and farther still.

Elspeth stared at the bald man, three times her size, covered in the finest herringbone wool—yards of it, she estimated—his purple four-in-hand held in place with a glittering diamond stick pin. She did not retreat, not one inch, but held completely still, her eyes riveted on his. She would not be the one to look away. He turned suddenly and swept his hand in a wide arc.

"I think she likes me! I think she's fallen under my spell! And she'll like my long, fat sausage too, won't she, boys?" He turned to look at her, bending his knees just a bit to grab his crotch and thrust his hips at her. The men in the crowd roared their approval.

The young man was pulling on his arm. "Schmitt! That's enough. Come away."

Elspeth speared him with her glare. "Make an escape now after your da's had his way and not paid her and hit her too? Coward!"

The muscles in the young man's neck stood out white against the red color of his face and throat. He leaned around the bald man. "He is *not* my father, miss. You should go before you are caught up in something ugly. Go."

"As if this is not ugly enough, a grown man in a fine suit hitting a woman on the stoop of her home!"

"It could get worse. Go!" he growled as the crowd shouted their appreciation at whatever crude comments Schmitt had just made.

"I'll see her—" Elspeth began and stopped abruptly as her

brother James shouldered past Schmitt and the young red-faced man. He put his hand under her arm, none too lightly, and turned her to go down the steps. Schmitt stepped in front of them.

"I saw her first, boy," he said. "Go on about your business."

"Come along, Elspeth," James said quietly without a glance at Schmitt.

"I'm sorry, miss," the young man said and reached out his hand as if hoping to shake hers. "Mr. Schmitt lost his head for a moment."

James leaned in and spoke quietly. "Don't touch my sister. Ever. And tell your friend to back out of our way."

"Or what, boy?" Schmitt asked and turned with a broad smile and a sweep of his arm to the crowd. "Or what?"

But other than a few whispered words and quick exchanges of coins, the young men crowded in the street were completely silent. They were all, as one, staring at her brother, clearly waiting for his response.

"You don't want to know," James said to Schmitt and turned his head to her. "Aunt Murdoch is worried about you."

"I highly doubt that," she said but held tight to her spot on the stoop. "This man has not paid this woman, and he hit her, James. It's not right."

"Unfortunately, she's in a business that is often dangerous. But we can do nothing for her. We're going, Elspeth."

The young man held out several paper bills. "Here. Give this to her, and then go before someone else is hurt."

Elspeth took the money and handed it to woman, still sitting on the doorway threshold, her hankie in the other woman's hand. The woman tried to return the hankie, now bloodstained, but Elspeth shook her head and smiled. "Do you have something for that?"

"Come on, Mary," a woman in a gauzy robe standing just inside the door said. "Come to the kitchen. We'll get some ice on it."

EXCERPT FROM THE BACHELOR'S BRIDE

Mary stood on shaky legs and let the woman inside help her until the door was closed. Elspeth turned to James. "We should be going," she said.

"Should we? You will be the death of me, Lizzie," James said with a quirk of his lips, using the childhood name that he knew she disliked.

They began down the steps together, and the boisterous men gathered around her and James as they finally skirted Schmitt, asking her brother all manner of questions, patting him on the back, and tugging on the brims of their caps to her or nodding in her direction. Elspeth glanced back at the young man, now watching her every movement. It was as if he was memorizing her features for some future inspection, and it made a chill run down her spine.

# EXCERPT FROM INTO THE EVERMORE

*Into the Evermore*

November 1842 Virginia

"Twenty dollars and you can have her. Don't make no never mind to me what you do with her. I just want to see the gold first."

The filthy-looking bearded man waved his gun in every direction as he spoke, including at the head of the young woman he held in his arms and at the three men in front of him. The trio all had handkerchiefs covering the lower part of their faces and hats pulled down tight, revealing six eyes now riveted to the pistol as it honed in on one random target after the other. The woman was struggling, although it was a pitiful attempt as she was clearly exhausted, and maybe hurt. The wind whipped through the trees, blowing the dry snow in circles around them. Beau Gentry watched the grim scene play out as he peered around a boulder down into a small ravine. He'd been propped against the sheltered rock, dozing, and thinking he'd best start a fire, when he heard voices below.

## EXCERPT FROM INTO THE EVERMORE

"Ain't paying twenty dollars in gold for some used-up whore," one of the masked men said.

The filthy man wrenched his arm tighter around the woman and put the gun to her temple. "Tell 'em, girly. Tell 'em you ain't no whore."

She shrank away from the barrel of the gun and moaned. "Please, mister. Let me go," she begged.

"Tell 'em you ain't no whore!"

She shook her head and pulled at the filthy man's arm around her waist. "I'm no fallen lady," she whispered. "I'm just, I'm just . . ." The woman went limp, and Beau thought she'd fainted but instead she vomited into the snow in front of her. He watched her choke and gag, bent over the man's arm, and that's when he realized she was barefoot.

Beau leaned back against the rock and checked his pistols and shotgun beside him. He hoped his horse wouldn't bolt from the tree she was loosely tied to when the bullets started to fly. It'd be a long walk back to Winchester if she did, especially as he'd most likely be carrying the woman. "Shit," he muttered. "Shit and damnation. She doesn't have any goddamn shoes on."

From his angle, he'd need to drop the three bandits with the two shells from the shotgun, and finish off any of them still breathing with one of his pistols. They'd be surprised and hopefully slow if the liquor smell floating on the wind meant anything. He was counting on the filthy man being hampered by the woman's struggling. He was hoping she didn't get shot in the cross fire, but then she'd be better off dead than facing what was in store for her if the filthy man was the victor. The argument over the gold was getting heated, he could hear, making this as good a time as any.

The snow fell away from the fur collar and trim of Beau's coat as he stood, lifted the shotgun to his shoulder, and aimed at the first man. He pulled the trigger, sighted in the second man, and pulled the second trigger right after the other, marching forward through brush and snow, letting the shotgun fall from his hands as he went. Two of the men dropped and the third fell to his knees, aiming his pistol at Beau as he did. Beau lengthened his stride, pulled a pistol from his waistband as he made the clearing, raised his left arm straight, and dropped the kneeling man to the ground with a shot to his face, letting the spent weapon fall to the ground. As he turned, he pulled his new fighting knife free of its scabbard and brought his right hand up, wielding a second pistol, side-stepping to get an angle on the filthy man.

"She's mine! You ain't getting her."

"Drop the gun."

"Twenty dollars in gold and you can have her!"

He wondered how much longer the woman would last. She was white-faced, except for the dirt, and her hair hung in clumps, matted together with blood. Her mouth was open in a silent scream. She raised and lowered her arms as if paddling in a pool of water. Most likely she was long past terrified and all the way to hysterical.

"Fine," Beau said. "You want twenty dollars?"

The filthy man nodded, and Beau dropped his knife in the snow and reached his hand in his pants pocket as if intending to retrieve a gold piece. The man lowered his weapon by an inch or so as his eyes followed Beau's hand, and in that moment Beau brought up his right hand and fired his weapon. The bullet tore through the man's neck, sending blood gushing into the snow as the man tumbled sideways, releasing the woman. She fell in the opposite direction, covered in splattered blood, clawing and crawling away from her captor, turning on her back and shoving off in the mud and snow with bleeding feet, pushing herself away. Her cry echoed in the silent cold night.

Beau pulled his knife from the snow, kicked away the filthy man's gun, and walked to where he lay, now writhing as he slowly drowned in his own blood. The hair on the back of Beau's neck stood and he turned. The last of the three men, missing part of his cheek and ear, had retrieved a loaded pistol from the belt of one of his companions and was now aiming it at Beau with shaking hands. Beau released the knife with a whip of his wrist, landing it dead center on the man's chest. He turned to the woman and watched as her eyes rolled back in her head and she crumbled the last four or five inches, until her back hit the forest floor.

Made in the USA
Coppell, TX
07 February 2022

73115443R00118